BEFORE I KNEW I LOVED YOU

Also by Toshikazu Kawaguchi

Before the coffee gets cold
Tales from the cafe
Before your memory fades
Before we say goodbye
Before we forget kindness

Toshikazu Kawaguchi

BEFORE I KNEW I LOVED YOU

Translated from the Japanese by Geoffrey Trousselot

PICADOR

First published 2026 by Picador
an imprint of Pan Macmillan
The Smithson, 6 Briset Street, London EC1M 5NR
EU representative: Macmillan Publishers Ireland Ltd, 1st Floor,
The Liffey Trust Centre, 117–126 Sheriff Street Upper,
Dublin 1 D01 YC43
Associated companies throughout the world

ISBN 978-1-0350-4629-4 HB
ISBN 978-1-0350-4630-0 PB

Originally published in Japan as ITOSHISA NI KIZUKANU UCHI NI
by Sunmark Publishing Inc., Tokyo, Japan in 2024
Japanese / English translation rights arranged with Sunmark Publishing, Inc.,
through Gudovitz & Company Literary Agency, New York USA

Translated from Japanese by Geoffrey Trousselot.

1 3 5 7 9 8 6 4 2

A CIP catalogue record for this book is available from the British Library.

Typeset in ITC Giovanni Std by Six Red Marbles UK, Thetford, Norfolk
Printed and bound in the UK using 100% Renewable Electricity by CPI Group (UK) Ltd

FSC
www.fsc.org
MIX
Paper | Supporting
responsible forestry
FSC® C116313

If you could go back, who would you want to meet?

Relationship map of characters

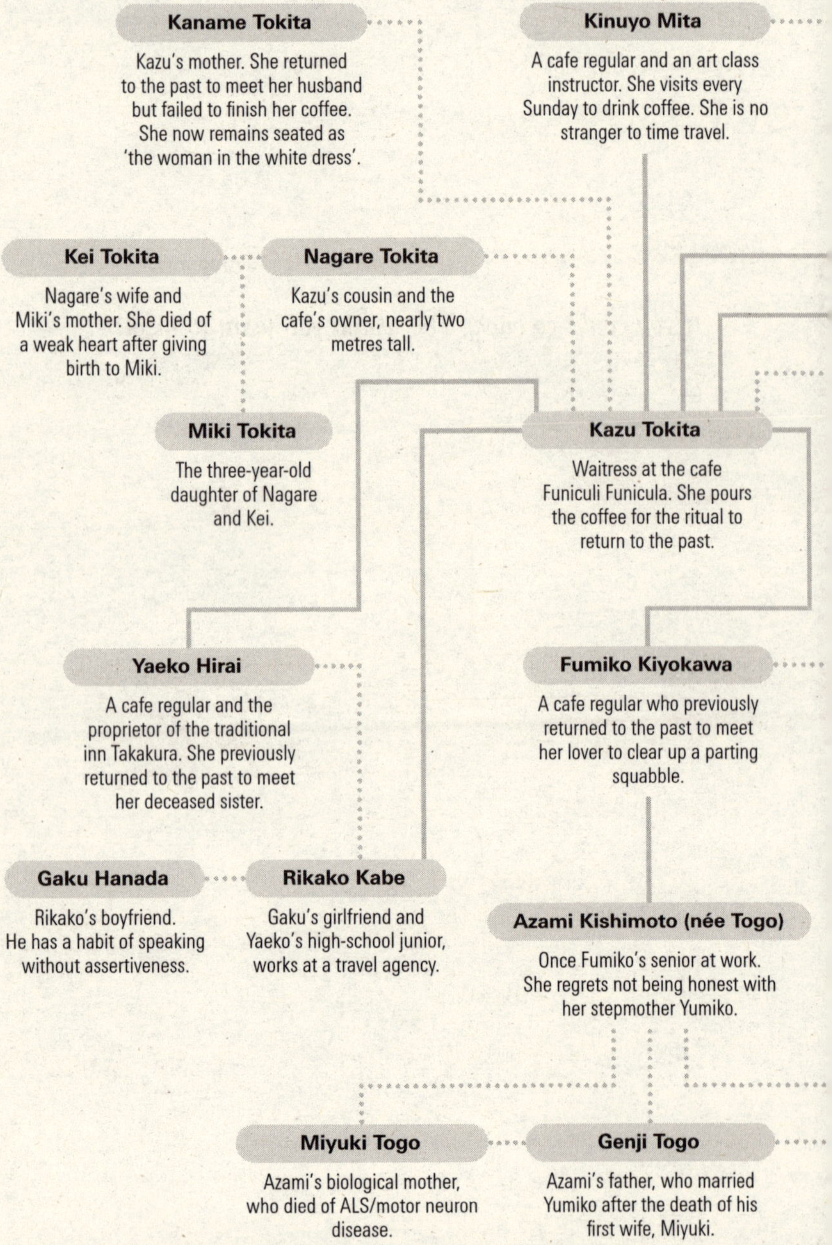

Yosuke Mita

Kinuyo's grandson

Ryutaro Suga

Tsuguo's father, a chef. He raised Tsuguo alone after divorcing and died of a heart condition.

customer

Tsuguo Suga

A junior-high student who visits Funiculi Funicula to meet his deceased father.

customer

friend

Koku Shintani

A world-travelling photographer who has feelings for Kazu.

Goro Katada

Currently working in Germany to achieve his dreams, he is in a long-distance relationship with Fumiko.

Misuzu Horie

Kanna's best friend, trying to help Tomokazu and Kanna get together.

Tomokazu Okishima

A university student who returned to the past to meet Kanna, his crush back in junior high school.

Kanna Ozaki

Tomokazu's classmate back in junior high school.

Shigeki Hayashida

Tomokazu's friend, who has a crush on Kanna.

Yumiko Togo

Azami's stepmother, who struggled to bond with Azami and died without reconciling.

CONTENTS

Prologue XI

I *The Runaway* 1

II *The Patient Man* 57

III *The Secret* 123

IV *The Father and Son* 189

Prologue

There is a mysterious rumour about a peculiar seat in a cafe tucked away somewhere in the city. They say that whoever sits on that chair can travel to a time of their choosing.

However, there are the following annoying and extremely frustrating rules:

1. You can only meet someone who has visited or will visit the cafe.
2. Nothing you say or do in the past will change the present.

3. The chair is already occupied, so you must wait for its current occupant to move.
4. Once in the past, you must remain sitting there, never getting up.
5. Your time is short. It lasts only until you finish the coffee, which you must do before it gets cold.

And yet, despite these rules, customers still come, hoping to take that journey.

The name of the cafe is Funiculi Funicula.

If you were given the chance, would you take that journey, having heard all those rules?

These are the stories of four heart-warming miracles that occurred in this mysterious cafe:

I The Runaway
II The Patient Man
III The Secret
IV The Father and Son

If you could return to that day, who would you go to meet?

I

The Runaway

October 1999

'Let go of me!'

A girl's voice echoed through Tenmonkan Arcade in Kagoshima.

The arcade was colourfully hued by countless neon lights. Cheerful laughter came from the many bars and restaurants.

Her name was Azami Togo, and she had been wandering the streets, alone, still in the tracksuit bottoms and jacket she was wearing when she impulsively fled from home.

'Wait!'

Azami's stepmother, Yumiko, was gripping her arm as the crowd teemed around them.

Yumiko's expression exposed her exhaustion, with deep bags under her eyes. She had been searching for Azami for three days and nights without a moment of sleep.

Azami bucked against Yumiko's grip, and as she wrenched free, the backpack she was holding was propelled into a man passing by, who spared her only a glance before being swallowed up into the sea of people.

Azami darted away from Yumiko, intending to flee into the crowd.

'Azami, wait! Please wait!' Yumiko desperately pushed through the throng. She could not lose Azami after finally finding her, she had to keep her in sight.

For those three days, Azami had been roaming the streets of Kagoshima. Imagining where she had wandered and how she had spent the past three days made Yumiko's heart ache.

The journey from her home in Miyazaki to Kagoshima a hundred and twenty kilometres away, even taking the cheapest expressway bus route, would have cost about three thousand yen, leaving Azami with barely any money, given she was a junior-high student with limited funds.

Judging by her pale complexion, she was undernourished. Early October nights were getting chilly, and Yumiko worried that if Azami got drenched in the rain she might catch a bad cold.

'Azami!'

'Stop following me!'

'Wait! Please!'

Azami's father, Genji, had refused to file a missing-person report, even though his daughter had run away, whereabouts unknown: he didn't want the community gossiping. 'She'll come back eventually,' he had insisted, making no effort to search for her. But Yumiko, after learning from Azami's friends where she had headed, searched tirelessly and finally found her.

'Azami!'

Yumiko once again grabbed hold of Azami's arm.

'Stop chasing me! Let me go!'

Driven by anger, Azami's flailing hand pushed Yumiko away. Yumiko lost her balance and fell to the ground.

'Just leave me be!'

Yumiko got up quickly, fearing that Azami might run away again.

'How can I just leave you alone? Why would you say that?'

Yumiko looked at Azami. Her sad eyes seemed to plead, *I've been so worried about you, searching everywhere . . .*

Azami averted her eyes with an exasperated expression as if loathing even to answer.

Yumiko approached her cautiously.

'Please, come back home. Your father is worried too, you know?'

'Oh, get real! I bet he's relieved that I'm gone. It's not just Dad, either. You think the same, don't you? You'd both be relieved with me out of the picture. You don't have to try to be my mum – we are not even blood-related!'

Relieved that she's gone? Who? Me?

Since she had married Azami's father, Yumiko had never once thought such a thing. On the contrary, she had been striving to be called 'Mum' as soon as possible.

What were all my efforts for?

Yumiko stared back at Azami in a daze. She felt the fatigue of three days and nights of relentless searching, the futility of her unrewarded efforts, and the burden of entering the family as an outsider, caught between father and daughter. Overcome by this mix of feelings, Yumiko felt all strength drain from her body. A voice in the back of her head spoke.

Perhaps I was forcing myself to believe this child was my own. After all, she isn't my daughter by birth.

Yumiko slowly closed her eyes. Tears fell for no single reason.

I might not be able to keep this up any more.

Yumiko's shoulder bag fell to the ground.

Azami glanced at the bag but didn't pick it up. Instead she turned to the downcast Yumiko.

'I'm not going back to that house,' she said and walked away.

Her expression was blank as she blended into Tenmonkan Arcade's night-time crowd.

January 2019

'I was fourteen years old at the time,' Azami recollected with a faraway look in her eyes. She was in Funiculi Funicula, a cafe rumoured to have a special seat that could take you back in time. Every once in a while, someone would call into the cafe with a wish to return to the past. Azami was one of them.

Listening to Azami's story were the cafe's waitress Kazu

Tokita and two regular customers, Kinuyo Mita and Fumiko Kiyokawa. Fumiko knew Azami from when she was a senior colleague in her company, a medical-equipment manufacturer. Fumiko was still a systems engineer there, while Azami had moved on, becoming a full-time stay-at-home wife.

Azami covered her face with her hands.

'It hit me for the first time just how much I hurt my mother, when a twist of fate landed me in the same situation,' she muttered, as if talking to herself. She had ended up being in her stepmother Yumiko's position because her husband had a child from an earlier relationship.

'Is your daughter also rebellious?' Kinuyo asked gently. She had been quietly listening to Azami's story from her seat at the counter.

She liked the coffee brewed by the cafe's owner, Nagare Tokita, and always dropped by at about this time on Sundays to drink a cup.

Azami quietly shook her head in response. 'My daughter has been calling me "Mum" from the start . . .' she managed to say before choking up.

Kinuyo and Fumiko waited silently for Azami to continue.

'I'm sorry,' Azami murmured, apologizing for crying despite her best intentions. Then, taking a shaky breath, she explained how she had often asked herself why she couldn't have been kinder to her stepmother – why she'd rebelled so much and never once called her 'Mum'. A couple of months ago, just when she began to reflect on these regrets, her father, who hadn't contacted her for over a decade, suddenly called to say that her mother had passed away.

Her voice caught again. 'I always thought there'd come a day when I could apologize . . .'

She was filled with remorse. Even though she had been young, she regretted her coldness towards her stepmother, and for never calling her 'Mum'.

'I am a terrible daughter . . .' Azami covered her face with her hands again and her shoulders shook.

In the quiet cafe, only her sobs and the ticking of the pendulum wall clock could be heard.

CLANG-DONG

In response to the doorbell ringing, Kazu glanced towards the entrance but chose not to offer the regular greeting of 'Hello, welcome,' perhaps in consideration of Azami's crying. The person entering was Yosuke, Kinuyo's grandson. The January air outside must have been very cold as his cheeks appeared chilled and bright red. Despite his fluffy down jacket, beanie, and scarf, he was wearing shorts that left his knees completely exposed.

He sneezed, then lingered at the entrance while sniffling.

Noticing him, Kinuyo looked at the three pendulum wall clocks. The one in the middle was about to strike four in the afternoon. 'Oh, is it that time already?' she said.

Yosuke came in to fetch her. A car was waiting for them outside.

Kinuyo glanced at Azami, then at Fumiko, her eyes asking, *Will she be all right?*

Fumiko blinked slowly in reply. *She'll be OK. I'll stay with her.*

With a brief nod to convey, *I'll leave it to you,* Kinuyo accepted Yosuke's hand and stepped down from the counter seat.

'Oh, by the way, Kazu dear,' she called out, as if just remembering.

Kazu was behind the counter polishing the silver cutlery. It's a task most places avoid, but with few customers, time wasn't an issue here. She paused and looked up.

'Have you thought about what I mentioned earlier?' Kinuyo enquired.

Kazu did not answer, revealing a troubled expression so unlike her usual stoic demeanour that it piqued Fumiko's curiosity.

'What's this about?' she interjected.

'Sensei asked me to help her with her art class.' Kazu referred to Kinuyo as 'sensei' because she had been learning painting in Kinuyo's art class since childhood. It was Kinuyo who had encouraged her to pursue art at university.

Normally reserved and distant, Kazu seemed to interact with Kinuyo more freely, as if they shared a special bond. Fumiko, who often observed them closely, once told Kazu that her relationship with Kinuyo was like that of parent and child. Kazu had said only, 'Thank you,' offering neither denial nor assent.

Kinuyo had been in poor health in recent years, repeatedly being admitted to and discharged from the general hospital near the cafe, and was now asking her to help with her art class.

'I am not getting any younger, and you never know what's around the corner, so . . . Please give it some thought.' Kinuyo bowed her head towards Kazu.

Still, Kazu remained silent, her expression clouded.

'Is it such a difficult decision?'

Fumiko voiced Kinuyo's feelings with this question, a directness Kinuyo herself could not manage.

'It feels like too much for me . . .'

Kazu was not normally someone who struggled to say no. She would tell anyone frankly if she couldn't do something. But because it was Kinuyo asking, she was showing her reluctance in her demeanour.

Noticing Kazu's conflicted expression, Fumiko found herself thinking again, *I don't know what happened back then, but it's clear that Kinuyo means a lot to Kazu.*

'There's really nothing to teach. As you know, the class just love getting together to draw,' said Kinuyo. She wouldn't have pressed Kazu if she didn't truly believe that only Kazu could be entrusted to preserve that atmosphere. And when Kazu's troubled expression remained, she added, 'Just being there is enough, Kazu dear.' And that was no empty reassurance; it was Kinuyo's honest conviction.

'That makes sense,' Fumiko added quickly, continuing to follow the conversation. She did not know much about the art class but agreed, *Kazu's mere presence would provide the students with a good sense of tension.*

'Right? So, please, if you could do that for me, Kazu.' Kinuyo clasped her hands together in a gesture of appeal and bowed her head again.

Kazu remained silent for a while, looking perplexed, but finally, with a resigned expression, she replied, 'OK, I'll do it.'

'Wonderful.' Kinuyo's face brightened instantly.

Spontaneously, Fumiko also joyfully exclaimed, 'Good on you, Kazu!'

Kazu had also softened her expression on seeing that both Kinuyo and Fumiko were pleased.

Kinuyo, led by Yosuke, stopped in front of the cash register to pay. She took out three hundred and eighty yen from her purse for the coffee and clinked it onto the change tray offered to her.

Kazu clattered on the register. 'The exact amount, thank you,' she said, picking up the money from the tray and placing it in the drawer.

'Thank you for the coffee, as always,' Kinuyo said, leaving the cafe with Yosuke.

CLANG-DONG

After Kinuyo left, silence once again enveloped the cafe. With no background music, all that could be heard was the ticking of the pendulum wall clocks.

Gosh, how should I go about this?

Fumiko was wondering how to begin. At least Azami was no longer crying. She had regained her composure during the exchange between Kinuyo and Kazu.

If only I had explained the rules properly before listening to Azami's story. Fumiko let out a small sigh.

It was Azami who had invited Fumiko for coffee. They had kept in touch since Azami left the company after marrying, but they hadn't met in a while.

Since Azami had chosen this cafe, Fumiko had anticipated that she wanted to return to the past. She had wondered who it was Azami wished to meet, and that question continued to intrigue her.

However, at this point in the conversation, she began to worry Azami didn't fully understand the cafe's rules. From the way things were going, it was clear that Azami wanted to meet her deceased stepmother.

It won't work if that's the case. I'm afraid this is leading up to a huge disappointment for Azami once I tell her.

Fumiko looked up at the ceiling, wishing that time would just stop, but her wish was not to be granted.

'Kiyo!' Azami called Fumiko by the nickname derived from her surname, Kiyokawa.

Fumiko blinked, as if pulled from deep thought. 'Yes?' Her voice wavered, lingering at the end as though she hadn't quite processed Azami's call. In truth, she had – she just needed an extra moment to brace herself. She knew precisely what Azami was about to bring up, but she still hadn't worked out how to explain her side of things.

Slowly turning round, Fumiko forced a smile.

'Kiyo,' Azami began, 'this is the cafe where you travelled back in time to meet Goro, isn't it?'

Azami was referring to something that had happened four years earlier. Fumiko had returned to the past to see Goro, who had also been Azami's colleague.

'Oh, um, yes, indeed it was. This cafe, yes.'

Unwilling to address the topic, her words came out like fruit salad. She fretted, *Maybe Azami has realized I don't want to talk about it,* and felt a chill inside.

Azami sensed Fumiko's unease.

She seems against the idea. Maybe she doesn't see any point in going back to meet Mum.

Still, she decided to speak up.

'Actually, I've been thinking about going back to meet my mother . . . What do you say?' she asked, lifting her head slowly to gauge Fumiko's reaction.

Yet doubts swirled inside her.

Am I being too impulsive? I only remembered this cafe and rushed here on a whim. And what would I even say once I met her? Besides, how is travelling to the past possible? It's all too strange to believe.

That was why she sought Fumiko's perspective – Fumiko had actually gone back in time.

In turn, Fumiko inferred from Azami's expression, *If she is asking for my opinion, she might not be completely decided on returning to the past. It might not be such a huge blow to hear that going back would be futile.*

Fumiko got up from her seat and stood in front of Azami.

'May I ask you just one thing?'

Azami's eyes widened in surprise, taken aback by Fumiko suddenly standing before her like that.

'What?'

'Did your stepmother ever come to this cafe?'

Azami was puzzled by Fumiko's question, not understanding her intent.

'No, she didn't . . .'

'I suspected as much,' said Fumiko with a knowing nod.

'What do you mean?'

Fumiko sighed.

'Stay with me and listen,' she began. 'You can go back to the past and you can return, but unfortunately, you won't be able to meet your stepmother.'

'What?' Azami stared at Fumiko with wide eyes, unable to immediately process those words. 'What do you mean?'

'There are rules.'

'Rules?'

'Yes.'

Fumiko detected a slight irritation in Azami's tone when she echoed 'Rules?' Part of her frustration would have been learning there were rules in her way, but most of it would have been fuelled by her unwillingness to accept Fumiko's statement: that she could not meet her stepmother. Fumiko understood this all too well.

I should have chosen my words more carefully. Perhaps if I had said 'might not be able to meet her' and then explained things from there . . .

Her lack of tact was Fumiko's least favourite trait. She now felt regretful that she had missed out in sharing a warm moment with Azami as she expressed her wish to meet her deceased stepmother.

Fumiko straightened her posture and met Azami's gaze.

'I'm sorry. I must not have explained things well enough,' she said, and she dipped her head in apology.

Azami regretted revealing her dissatisfaction so openly. It must have felt to Fumiko like an affront.

When upset feelings lead to conflict, misread emotions are often to blame. Misunderstandings can occur in any relationship – between close friends, colleagues, parents and children, or siblings. Even intimate partners aren't immune to it. Because emotions are invisible, interpreting others' feelings based on their words and gestures is challenging. We tend to imagine what we can't see. Moreover, the way we perceive the emotions of others is heavily influenced by the state of our own minds.

However, Fumiko's gesture of apology was enough for Azami to realize that she was being hasty.

Kiyo is trying to tell me something important, yet I got upset just over the fact that she said I couldn't meet my mother.

She took a deep breath to calm herself, letting her gaze wander as if searching through her memories from four years ago.

Thinking about it now, when Kiyo sent me an email about her meeting with Goro, who had gone to America, I think she wrote some things about the cafe.

Azami recalled how she hadn't believed what Fumiko said about 'returning to the past'. She delved deeper into her memories.

Perhaps she did mention something about rules.

She strained to recall what Fumiko had said back then, but the details simply wouldn't come. All she remembered was that Fumiko had visited a mysterious cafe and returned to the past. From that alone, she assumed that going to this cafe would allow her to travel back in time too.

She realized it was wrong of her to react so impulsively.

'No, Kiyo, you have nothing to apologize for. I was the one acting rashly,' she said, softening her expression. 'I'll calm down. Could you continue your explanation?'

Fumiko felt relieved to see Azami's irritation fade. She also decided to focus on keeping her emotions in check and staying as calm and succinct as possible.

'All right,' she said. 'There are several rules for time travel in this cafe. One of them is that you can't meet anyone who hasn't been here before.'

Azami's eyes widened. *She sounds so serious, there is no way she's joking.* 'Does that mean I won't be able to meet my mother?' She turned to Kazu standing behind the counter – she needed to hear it from someone who worked there. 'Excuse me, is that true?'

'Yes,' Kazu confirmed without hesitation.

'Oh . . . OK,' Azami replied softly, lowering her gaze. She

realized she'd come here without knowing this crucial rule, and fighting the embarrassment rising inside her, she lifted her head again and asked, 'So why can't I just go and visit her?'

Sensing Kazu hesitate, Fumiko answered in her place. 'To be precise, you can go back to the past, but you cannot just go and visit your stepmother.'

'But why?' Azami pressed.

'Because even if you return to the past, you can't leave the cafe,' Fumiko explained. The actual rule was that you must remain in your seat, but she simplified it to highlight what mattered most to Azami.

Azami slumped. 'Really? I can't even do that?'

'It's one of the rules,' Fumiko said quietly, lowering her eyes. She regretted not explaining it more thoroughly when Azami first called – *If I were in her position, I'd be upset I wasn't told sooner.* She half expected Azami to voice exactly that complaint.

But in response, Azami remained calm. 'Is that so . . . Well, it can't be helped.' She sighed deeply.

Fumiko felt a pang of guilt remembering how badly Azami had wanted to meet her mother. 'I'm so sorry, Azami,' she said, looking down.

'Why are you apologizing, Kiyo?' Azami asked gently.

'I never wanted to raise your hopes,' Fumiko murmured.

'Fumiko, it's not like that,' Azami said, causing Fumiko to look up again. 'When you first told me about this cafe, I'm sure you explained everything, but it sounded like nonsense to me then. I only half listened, not fully grasping that the rules were so important. Later, I just assumed I could meet my mother.' Azami paused, out of breath from her hasty delivery, then said with a gentle smile, 'That's on me, not you.' Dropping her gaze, her voice trembled as she added, 'It's too late now. If only I'd reconciled with her sooner . . .'

The disappointment weighed heavily in Azami's words. Left without a response, Fumiko could only stare at the slowly turning wooden ceiling fan.

CLANG-DONG

The ring of the doorbell echoed through the silent cafe.

Without saying, 'Hello, welcome,' Kazu simply glanced at the central pendulum wall clock. Fumiko thought Kazu was probably being considerate of the disheartened Azami. At the same time, she was hoping this new customer might lighten the mood.

'Kazu, isn't that a customer?' she remarked. But she immediately thought, *What am I even saying?* Obviously, that was something Kazu would notice without needing to be told.

Nevertheless, Kazu obligingly turned her gaze towards the entrance and said, 'Hello, welcome.'

'We're back!'

It was Nagare Tokita, holding his three-year-old daughter, Miki.

Miki liked clinging to the chest of nearly two-metre-tall Nagare. Having never fallen, even when he inadvertently let go, Miki enjoyed calling herself a 'clingy bug' in this situation.

'Oh, it's Nagare . . .' said Fumiko, sighing because it was not a customer.

'Hello, welcome,' said Nagare to Azami. 'Are you a friend of Fumiko's?'

'Ah, yes. She used to be my senior colleague,' said Fumiko, answering for Azami.

'I see, nice to meet you,' Nagare said with a courteous tilt of the head.

'Likewise. I'm Azami Kishimoto.'

Azami stood up and bowed. While greeting him, her eyes widened in surprise. *I've never seen such a tall person before.*

'Oh, don't mind me. Have a relaxing time,' Nagare replied and then placed Miki on one of the counter seats before going to the kitchen.

'Hello, Miki sweetie,' said Fumiko, trying to engage with Miki. Miki, however, ignored her and continued looking straight ahead. 'Miki dear?'

Fumiko was perplexed by Miki's non-response.

Nagare, now dressed in his cook's uniform, came out of the kitchen imitating the vibration of an incoming mobile phone call.

Fumiko blinked her large eyes as she looked at him, and he apologetically squinted his eyes almost to a thread and winked.

'*Vrrr, vrrr, vrrr.* Hey, it's a call from Ms Fumiko! *Vrrr, vrrr, vrrr,*' he said, handing Miki a toy mobile phone.

Fumiko was bewildered. She observed the exchange between father and daughter, and waited for Miki's next move.

Miki pretended to press the call button. 'Hello? Who's calling please?' she asked, holding the toy phone to her ear.

Nagare was standing behind Miki with his hands together imploring, *Please play along with her*, and Fumiko took the hint.

She hastily took her phone out of her shoulder bag and put it to her ear.

'Hello,' she responded.

'Who is this?'

'It's Fumiko.'

'Which Fumiko?'

'Um . . .' Fumiko, not sure whether Miki even knew another Fumiko, tentatively replied, 'It's Fumiko Kiyokawa.'

'Ah, Fumiko Kiyokawa? It's been a while.'

'Yes, it has.'

Fumiko, pleased with the conversation so far, gave Nagare an OK sign, to which he responded with a wry smile.

'And how have you been?' continued Miki.

'I'm well. How are you, Miki?'

'Oh, don't worry about me.'

Miki's out-of-the-blue reply was too much. Fumiko burst into laughter.

'Hey, when Ms Fumiko asks if you're well, you should say you're well!' interjected Nagare, unable to stay out of the conversation any longer. This added to the hilarity, making Fumiko double over with laughter. Azami, watching from the side, also burst out laughing.

'Well, anyway, take care, *bip* . . .' and with that, Miki ended the call.

Despite being hung up on, Fumiko couldn't stop laughing.

'Fumiko Kiyokawa is well,' Miki declared with a smug expression.

'Stop calling her just Fumiko! You should say Ms Fumiko!'

'Ms.'

'Ms Fumiko!'

'Ms Fumiko.'

Amused and somewhat exasperated by Miki's antics, Nagare let out a huge sigh.

'You'll have to excuse us,' he said apologetically to Fumiko.

'No, it's OK. She's cute, isn't she? Little Miki is really something.'

Fumiko's exuberance puzzled Nagare. She continued to heap praise on Miki. 'She's wonderful, so wonderful.' She was happy because Miki's arrival on the scene had managed to dispel the stifling atmosphere that had been hanging in the room.

Miki saved the mood.

Fumiko truly believed that.

'Hmmm, I wonder if someone else will call me?'

'That's enough. No more calls today,' Nagare muttered, leaning against the kitchen entrance.

'Why?'

'Because it's a rule that you can only talk on the phone once a day.'

'Is there a rule?'

Miki tilted her head quizzically.

'Ah, how cute!' Fumiko, exclaimed involuntarily, looking at Miki.

As for Nagare, he was thinking, *She's becoming more and more like her.*

'OK, it's over,' he said with a sigh, reaching out his hand to take the toy phone back from Miki.

Nagare was thinking about Kei Tokita, his wife and Miki's mother, who passed away shortly after giving birth to Miki. Like her daughter, Kei was free-spirited and cheerful, often laughing with her big, sparkling eyes; the complete opposite to Nagare, who was reserved and not good at socializing, Kei was loved by everyone for her charming demeanour. Miki was increasingly resembling her mother.

Nagare was not troubled by this; rather, he found it delightful. However, he was astonished at how his growing daughter was resembling his wife more and more each day, without anyone teaching her. Moreover, Miki was even more free-spirited and carefree than her mother, and he was swept along by her daily. Because Kei was an adult, when Nagare was tired, she didn't involve him, but Miki was a child and constantly drew him into her world. No matter how delicious a food is, if you eat the same thing every meal, day after day, you can get tired of it.

The best approach is to moderately engage with Miki without getting too caught up in her pace, Nagare thought.

Fumiko watched carefully, wary that Miki might throw a tantrum.

But, agreeing obediently, Miki said, 'It can't be helped, it's the rule.'

Wow! Even though she's so young, little Miki already understands that she can't break the rules!

Impressed by this, Fumiko watched as Miki handed the toy back to Nagare.

'Ah!' Fumiko exclaimed unexpectedly.

'What?'

'What is it?'

Startled, Azami and Nagare called out to Fumiko simultaneously.

'Kazu, might that not work?' Fumiko said with eyes sparkling.

Nagare and Azami were completely clueless as to what Fumiko had in mind, but Kazu seemed to get her drift.

'Yes, it's possible,' she replied.

'It's possible, right?' said Fumiko, pressing her point loudly, nearly leaping over the counter in her excitement.

In stark contrast, Kazu replied with a soft 'Yes.'

'What are you talking about?' Nagare asked.

Ignoring him, Fumiko sat down opposite Azami.

'Azami!'

'What is it?'

'I think it's possible after all!'

'I'm sorry, I don't follow.'

'I think you can talk! You definitely can't meet your

stepmother face to face if you go back. But I think you can talk to her!'

'What? Really?'

'You can talk on the phone.'

Azami looked puzzled.

'When you go back, you just need to phone her,' Fumiko said enthusiastically. She was pleased with her brilliant idea.

'I see.'

But even after hearing Fumiko's clever plan, Azami was still gloomy.

She could imagine talking over the phone and was genuinely impressed by Fumiko, who – inspired by the toy phone – had thought she could go back in time and call her stepmother. Considering that she couldn't actually meet her mother, even if she returned to the past, perhaps she should be happy just to be able to talk.

Yet a smouldering thought lingered: *I really wanted to meet and apologize.*

Fumiko was quick to pick up on Azami's feelings.

'Sorry, maybe it wouldn't be the same with just a phone call,' she said. Embarrassed by her own excitement, she lowered her head.

'Sorry, sorry, I didn't mean it like that,' Azami said, hurriedly waving her hands.

Her reluctance to speak with her stepmother over the phone was not just because she wanted to apologize in person.

'With a phone call, you know, you can't see the person's face, so . . .'

'So?'

'It's scary.'

'Scary?'

'If only we could meet, I could see her face and understand what she thinks of me without her saying a word. She might be angry because we haven't spoken in years, and she might wonder why I've returned now. But those feelings would show, right? I think I'd realize how much I've hurt her just by looking at her . . .'

Azami paused, gazing at her hands. The cafe was almost completely still, with only the ceiling fan turning slowly. As if time itself had stopped, no one moved an inch until Azami's fingertips moved slightly. Fumiko even forgot to breathe as she awaited Azami's next words.

'I believe I deserve to feel guilty for hurting my mother. I caused her pain for many years – I was a terrible daughter. So, I need to truly understand how much she suffered. I need to be blamed.'

'But . . .' Fumiko wanted to say, *I think you've suffered enough, and I don't believe your stepmother wants to blame you!*

But then she hesitated, thinking, *If someone other than Goro had told me about his true feelings after he went to America, would I have believed them?*

She swallowed the words she was about to speak.

I wouldn't be able to believe those words myself. Right now, to her, I am an outsider – they're just my speculations and mere words of comfort. That's why she needs to hear it directly from her step-mother. No, she absolutely must! Otherwise, she'll go through life without ever knowing her stepmother's true feelings, dragging the weight of the past with her.

Leaning forward emphatically, Fumiko said, 'But you won't know whether your stepmother was angry with you unless you ask her directly!'

I'm probably stepping over the line in my meddling, but it's justified.

Fumiko, looking at Azami, who now was wide-eyed, continued.

'You should go back, Azami – you need to hear what your stepmother truly felt. I understand it's scary, and you might be shocked by her true feelings, but isn't that OK? Instead of living with all that worry and uncertainty because you never knew how she felt, it's definitely better to go back, talk to her, and put your mind at ease!' Fumiko rushed through her words with earnest eyes.

Azami burst into laughter because Fumiko had so accurately pinpointed what was in her heart.

'Did I say something funny?' Fumiko blinked.

'Sorry, sorry. I laughed because you're so right, Kiyo.'

'How?'

'Maybe, deep down, I'm just afraid to know my mother's true feelings. I said I wanted to go back and see her, but when I learned I couldn't meet someone who hadn't visited this cafe, I felt secretly relieved. By pretending I was going to see her, I was trying to escape – even just a little – from the guilt of having treated her so terribly. I never truly believed I could return to the past anyway.'

'Azami, we are not lying to you. You really can go back in time in this cafe!' Fumiko looked to Nagare and Kazu behind the counter for backup.

'Yes, I know you aren't lying, Kiyo. It's me, not you. I guess . . . deep down I'm scared and finding excuses not to go back.'

'Azami . . .'

'Aren't I pathetic! Kiyo, you seem to care more about my life than I do. If I'm serious about apologizing, a phone call or anything will do. I actually do want to know my mother's true feelings, so I definitely should go back, shouldn't I?'

Azami waited for Fumiko's response.

Fumiko was about to say, *You should go*, but she chose not to.

'That's for you to decide, Azami,' she said instead.

Azami took a moment to confront her own feelings and replied with a smile, 'So true.'

'Ah, but there's just one problem . . .' Fumiko began. Seconds after Azami finally decided in her heart, *I'll go*, Fumiko was looking at her with a grim expression.

'Problem? What?'

'When you go back, you'll be sitting over there, where the woman in the white dress is. The very first thing you must do is borrow the cafe's phone.'

As Fumiko said this, she looked at Kazu and Nagare behind the counter.

'Just ask. You don't need to give a reason. That would be a waste of time. When you return to the past, you only have as long as it takes for you to drink the cup of coffee, and you have to finish it before it cools down completely.'

'That's a rule as well?'

'Yes! So when you go back, you mustn't waste even a second! One of those two will lend it to you without needing to know why.'

'Oh, OK.'

'And may I continue? What I'm about to say is important, so please listen carefully.' Fumiko leaned forward and lowered her voice.

'Once the phone is in your hand, call your stepmother straight away. There's no time to hesitate. From my experience, it's about eight minutes until the coffee cools, at most ten.'

'Eh?' Azami exclaimed in surprise. 'It's that short?'

'That's all you get.'

Azami looked into Fumiko's eyes; she was clearly telling the truth.

'All right, if that's all I've got . . .' she replied softly.

What if I hesitate when the time comes to make the call?

As if to dispel her worries, Fumiko added, 'So, when you go back, borrow the phone immediately and make the call before you hesitate!'

She kept her face stern to stress her point.

'OK, I got it,' Azami answered while looking away from Fumiko.

'And now I'm going to tell you the most important point.'

'There's more?'

'Yes, there is.'

'Well, what is it?'

'Even if you make the call with no hesitation . . .'

'Even if I do?'

'Your stepmother may not be at home.'

'Oh . . .'

Calling her stepmother would be all in vain if she wasn't there, and because Azami hadn't been in contact with her family since leaving home, she didn't know her mobile phone number.

'So, if you go back, you should choose a time when your stepmother is most likely to answer the phone, perhaps even late at night.'

'Oh, I didn't think of that.'

While impressed by Fumiko's precise advice, the challenge of talking to her stepmother after going back was daunting.

Maybe she'll answer the phone, maybe she won't. But if she does, will she even listen? What can you say in less than ten minutes? If I apologize, is that for my sake or hers? How would my mother feel?

The anxiety and doubt kept her heart feeling perpetually unsettled.

Azami thought of past events.

Following the incident at the Tenmonkan shopping arcade in Kagoshima, she wandered to another town, where she was finally picked up by the police and escorted home.

Even after returning home, Azami and Yumiko's relationship remained unrepaired, with Azami continuing to ignore her stepmother. When she came home from school each day she hastily retreated to her room. She even took her meals there. She never responded to Yumiko's attempts at conversation, unless absolutely necessary, in which case she would converse through jotted notes.

Once, when her form teacher, who knew about her father's remarriage, asked, 'How are things going with your new stepmother?' she replied dismissively, 'I don't think of her as my mother.'

Although Azami continued to ignore her, Yumiko devotedly fulfilled her role as mother. Nevertheless, Azami's attitude did not change even after she got a job and left home.

And life went on.

After she married and began raising a child not biologically hers, just like Yumiko, Azami realized, *I must have made life a living hell for Mum back then. If I'm given the chance, I want to apologize properly. She might not forgive me, but I need to try.*

She began to feel regret. Though she wanted to apologize, she thought, *Dad and Mum must have their own new child now. Anyway, they've probably forgotten about me. If I suddenly showed up, they might ask coldly why I bothered coming back.* And so she found it hard to make contact.

Azami learned of Yumiko's death about two months before visiting the cafe Funiculi Funicula.

Calling her on the phone, her father had said, 'At least come to the funeral.'

As she watched the smoke rise from the crematorium's chimney she reflected, *In the end, I never apologized.*

Strangely, no tears came.

Somewhere inside, Azami realized she had given up on repairing her relationship.

It's pointless now. I can't change the past. I can't undo what I've done. I was a terrible daughter, that's all.

The funeral ended and by the time she returned to her childhood home the sun was setting. For the first time in many years she walked slowly down the corridor leading from the entrance. With each step, the softly reverberating creak of the wooden floor emphasized the stillness of the house.

The Buddhist altar room was at the end of the hallway.

I'll say hello to Dad and then leave right away.

With her mind filled with childhood memories, she carefully avoided the floor's creaky spots as she made her way to the altar room. The scent of incense hit her.

Upon reaching the altar room, she hesitated to slide open the door.

'Dad?' she called out in a soft voice.

'Hmm?'

The responding voice was weak. Even with the cardboard of the fusuma door between them, she could tell he was facing the altar.

'I'm going home now . . .'

'Oh, OK.'

'Will you be all right? You won't be on your own, will you?'

she asked, though she thought, *Please don't ask me to stay . . .* and loathed herself for her insincere words.

'I'm fine.'

'OK.'

Even after hearing her father's response, Azami remained immobile in front of the fusuma door for a moment, unsure whether she should really just leave.

'Your mother never wanted to have more children.'

Her father's voice was quiet as if he was talking to himself.

Azami thought she must have misheard.

'What did you just say?'

'She said because you would always be the only child . . .'

'How can I believe that?'

In shock, Azami slid open the door.

Without replying, her father slowly rose and came into the hallway. Watching him ascend the stairs, Azami noticed a certain odd emptiness about the overly quiet house.

It had been over a decade since she left home. If her father and Yumiko had had children after that, they would be in upper elementary or junior high school by now. Azami walked from the altar room across the hallway, looking around the house.

She moved from the living room to the entrance. *That's strange . . .* She had thought it odd that there was no sign of the children at the funeral either. *Surely there would be shoes.*

But there weren't. Even in the shoe cabinet, the only shoes

were those belonging to her father and Yumiko. *But that makes no sense.*

She hesitantly climbed the stairs to visit her old room. If her father and Yumiko had children, the room would have been cleared out long ago.

But it wasn't. It was exactly as she had left it.

'I thought we should pack your things away, but your mother objected. That was the only time I ever fought with her after remarrying,' her father said.

He had entered her room before her. It was then that Azami looked properly at her father's face for the first time since she entered the family residence.

Who would want to see the face of such a terrible daughter? she had assumed.

But her father was smiling kindly.

'Welcome back. I'm sure your mother would be happy that you've come home,' he said.

On hearing those words, Azami collapsed to her knees and sobbed loudly.

Thinking about all those days of regretting what she could not amend, she could do nothing but cry.

Flap.

The sound of the woman in the white dress clapping her book shut snapped Azami back to reality.

'Oh,' she gasped as the woman in the white dress rose from

her seat. *That must be where I sit to go back to the past.* She looked questioningly at Fumiko.

Yes, it is. Fumiko, too, conveyed this with only her eyes; she had been busy thinking of ways to maximize Azami's chances of having that conversation.

I wish we had a bit more time. As Fumiko was thinking this with a remorseful expression, the woman in the white dress started to walk. It is commonly said that Japanese ghosts do not have feet, but the woman in the white dress did. Even though she had feet, she made no sound as she walked. Her legs moved as they should, but rather than rising and falling with each step, she glided across the room, passing between them, and heading towards the toilet.

The cafe fell silent once again.

Fumiko looked at the seat where the woman in the white dress had been sitting. Following her gaze, Azami looked too.

'Azami, the seat is vacant now,' Fumiko said as if testing how Azami was feeling.

Instead of replying, Azami looked back at Fumiko, who was gazing past her to where the woman in the white dress had gone. Azami felt Fumiko's look was saying, *Once she returns, the opportunity will be lost.*

'I take it we have little time to waste?'

Fumiko was reluctant to say anything in response. It is when pressed for time that people make the poorest judgements. However, trying not to rush her, she crafted her reply carefully.

'As you say, yes.'

What should I do?

Azami could not hide her agitation at suddenly having to decide whether to accept this opportunity or let it pass, but before she knew it, she found herself standing in front of the empty seat, as if drawn there by forces unknown.

'Still no second thoughts?' Kazu asked in a calm, measured tone, standing behind her.

Azami kept her gaze fixed on the seat, saying nothing. Kazu, indifferent to whatever decision Azami would reach, simply needed to know – if Azami chose to go back in time, there would be preparations to make.

After a brief pause, Azami spoke. 'I'll go.'

In that simple statement lay the realization that although she had no idea whether her stepmother would pick up the phone if she went back, she nevertheless knew for certain she would regret not trying.

'All right then.' Kazu quietly disappeared into the kitchen.

While staring at the seat that would take her back, Azami called out to Fumiko.

'So, I just sit down, right?'

'Yes.'

Azami took a deep breath and eased her way in between the chair and the table.

'I'm praying for you,' Fumiko added.

Even if Azami went back in time, whether her stepmother would answer the phone was outside her control, just a matter of chance. At this point, praying was all she could offer. Her words of support left Azami feeling grateful, and prompted her to confess something she could no longer hold in. Straightening her posture, she said, 'To be honest, I'm still afraid to speak to my mother.'

What? Fumiko stopped breathing for a moment.

Looking into her eyes, Azami could plainly see her confusion.

She continued.

'I'm almost ashamed to say it, but part of me hopes she won't pick up. I'm afraid because although I never contacted her, even once, here I am suddenly planning to – and I don't know what to say.'

Of course, if Azami returned from her trip to the past and reported that she was unable to speak to her stepmother, Fumiko would never criticize her. But as it was such a precious opportunity, she desperately hoped Azami would come out of it without regrets. Just as she was contemplating whether she should voice her thoughts, Azami continued.

'It's funny, but I now find myself loving the mother I used to hate so much.'

'Oh, Azami . . .'

In a voice that was gradually turning more tearful, Azami continued.

'If she were still alive, I'd do anything for her. I'd show her respect and say thank you to my mother, who called me her only daughter and forever waited for me. At the very least, I want to say those words.'

Azami broke off there. She covered her mouth to stifle her sobs and her shoulders shook. *Even if my mother truly hated me, that's OK. I want to tell her how I feel.* She clenched her teeth and looked up.

'Are you ready?'

Without being noticed, Kazu had returned and was standing right beside her.

'Ah, yes,' Azami hurriedly replied. She took a paper napkin from the table to wipe her wet cheeks.

Kazu took a pure white coffee cup from a silver tray and placed it in front of Azami.

'I will now pour your coffee,' she said.

Azami was captivated by the way Kazu placed the cup on the table. Her movement was so refined, so utterly devoid of waste, that even if she repeated it a hundred times it would be the same each time.

Kazu began her explanation.

'Your journey to the past begins from the moment I pour the coffee into the cup, and you can only remain there until you have drunk the coffee, and you must finish it before it has completely cooled.'

According to Fumiko, her time there would last about eight minutes, ten at most. Of course, she thought it short, but the time for hesitation was over.

'Yes, please proceed,' Azami declared.

Seemingly satisfied with Azami's resolve, Kazu lifted the silver kettle from the tray. Fumiko looked on in quiet hope, wishing Azami every success.

'Remember then . . .' Kazu paused to take a breath. 'Before the coffee gets cold.'

As her words echoed through the quiet cafe, a tension began to grow in the air. Azami felt her heart rate accelerate. Kazu raised the kettle and poured coffee into the cup with ceremonial grace. To calm her mind, Azami focused intently on the coffee filling the cup.

Once I return to the past, I must borrow a phone and call home at once. There will be no time to waste. Then, if my mother answers . . .

Upon contemplating this, she realized the coffee had filled the cup. A plume of steam unexpectedly spiralled above the surface and began rising.

'Ah!'

Feeling as if she were being carried by the steam, Azami shrieked involuntarily. She suddenly realized her body was turning into steam and also beginning to rise.

'Kiyo!'

Instinctively, she called out to Fumiko for help, but looking around, everything was descending around her; Fumiko had fallen from sight. Helpless, Azami could only surrender to it, becoming one with the steam and passing into the ceiling.

Mummy . . .

As Azami's consciousness drifted far away, she recalled the day of her biological mother's funeral.

My biological mother's name was Miyuki, meaning beautiful snow, and true to her name, she had a snowlike complexion. Miyuki had developed motor neuron disease, which progressed to lengthy hospitalization near the end. But she passed away peacefully at home, watched over by me and my father.

I was told that ALS is a neurodegenerative disease that gradually kills motor neurons, manifesting first as loss of muscle control, and then as muscle weakness and atrophy. For my biological mother, the first noticeable symptom was speech impairment. Although research is still ongoing, and clinical trials for new treatments and drugs are being conducted, I haven't yet heard of a cure that completely stops its progression.

As an elementary-school student, I had never before experienced such a sorrow as my biological mother's death. Likewise, it was a huge blow for my father. I remember he was even more grief-stricken and exhausted than I was. Seeing him like that, I could only think, *I mustn't upset him more.*

Being the only child, I took on household chores by myself around the time my real mother was diagnosed with ALS. However, after she passed away, I gave up my club activities and took over all household responsibilities, from preparing meals to doing the laundry and cleaning. I think I was trying to protect our home for my father and myself, believing it would make him happy.

This continued for about six months, and my father began to recover bit by bit. I was fully prepared to struggle through life with my father, just the two of us.

After not much more than a year, however, my father introduced my stepmother to me: 'This is your new mother, Yumiko.'

Yumiko was a childhood friend of Miyuki, and my father

had been acquainted with her through that. Apparently, I had met her several times before, but I had no memories of it. Without me having any say in it, we were officially recorded as family.

Looking back, my father probably felt sorry for me because I had had to give up club activities to focus on looking after things at home. Perhaps my form teacher had mentioned something to him.

'Leave the household chores to Yumiko,' he would say every time he saw me. This, of course, stemmed from his kindness, something I understand now, but couldn't at the time.

But can't you see how hard I've been working?

I felt my stepmother had stolen my job. She must have wished I would spend more time as a child, but that was a sentiment my heart could not fathom.

It was as if my father had told me, 'You can't replace Miyuki.' I felt nothing but sadness. My stepmother's arrival left me devoid of purpose, and this eventually led me to feel I no longer belonged.

Maybe it would be better if I wasn't here.

Back then, I saw leaving home as my only choice. Had I had the courage to talk to my father, had I had the strength to accept my stepmother's viewpoint rationally, I might have had a completely different future. But I didn't listen to my father, and I had no room in my heart to accept my stepmother.

All three of us were desperate to place family first, my father in his way, my stepmother in hers, and me in mine. But I was unable to express that sentiment. Neither I nor my parents were able to convey our true feelings to each other back then, inadvertently creating an unhappy situation that none of us wanted.

I should have mustered up a little more courage to say that I wanted us three to be happy together.

June 2015

'Oh, hello! Welcome, welcome.'

The buoyantly cheerful voice roused Azami.

Behind the counter was a woman with large, round eyes smiling radiantly at Azami, who was in the seat that could take her back in time. It was Kei Tokita, the wife of Nagare Tokita, the owner of the cafe.

Who is that?

Azami nodded to Kei and looked around the cafe. Located two floors below street level, it was windowless, making it impossible to tell if it was day or night. The three pendulum wall clocks were no help either, as they all showed different times, leaving Azami unsure whether she had even returned to the past.

Then Kei asked, 'From the future?'

Although Azami and Kei were meeting for the first time, and their relationship was merely that of customer and staff, Kei's tone was as casual as if speaking to a friend. However, it was not at all unpleasant, for her unguarded nature and innocent, childlike charm were endearing.

'Er, yes.'

Though still somewhat sceptical, Azami decided it was best to accept that she was back in the past. If she believed Fumiko, her time before the coffee got cold would be very brief. Doubts would waste it.

Feeling the coffee cup, she realized the coffee had already cooled. Though this was unexpected, she concluded, *There is no need to panic just yet.*

She remembered what Fumiko had told her, and got to the point at once.

'Could I borrow your phone for a moment?'

'Our phone?' Kei blinked, repeatedly.

Seeing Kei's reaction, Azami thought: *Was I too abrupt, perhaps?* Explanation was needed. 'Well, actually—'

But Kei cut her off. 'A phone, gotcha. I'll be right back.' She disappeared from sight and Azami was taken aback by the swiftness of her departure.

Then Kei returned with a cordless phone in her hand.

'Here you go.'

'Ah, thank you.'

Although Fumiko had assured Azami that no explanation would be necessary, Azami still hadn't expected Kei – whom she'd just met – to hand her a phone without a single comment. Kei covered her mouth with her hand, as if to signal, 'I won't ask anything.' In addition to indicating that she understood how urgent the situation was, Kei's gesture was a gentle nudge to Azami to hurry with her call. It was also utterly disarming, and Azami warmed to Kei immediately, thinking that once she returned to the future, she would love to be friends.

'Thanks, I'll make the call right now.'

Azami nodded gratefully and started to enter the home phone number on the handset.

'Kei, is there something wrong?'

Nagare appeared from the back room. He must have come to see what Kei was up to – after all, she'd rushed in, grabbed the cordless phone, and hurried back to the cafe.

But Azami hadn't noticed his arrival. He observed Azami seated at the usual table, eyes fixed intently on the handset, and Kei covering her mouth.

'I see,' he muttered. Not because he understood everything, but because he realized now wasn't the time to interrupt, and whatever reason Kei had for covering her mouth, it wasn't important enough to question.

Yet Azami's hand was poised above the key pad. Had she already dialled the number, she would have been holding the handset to her ear. But she was just staring at the handset, motionless.

Wait a minute! What if . . . What if what Dad told me about Mum was a lie?

On the day of the funeral, Azami heard from her father that Yumiko had not wanted children.

Indeed, she saw no evidence that they had children, either at the funeral or inside her family home. There was simply no reason to doubt her father's words. But why didn't they? What if her father hadn't told the entire truth? Azami resented her imagination in such moments. The real reason they had no more children might have been completely different. Her father might have lied to avoid hurting her.

If it was a lie, that would change everything. *I'm only strong enough to make this call because I'm assuming Mum loved me.* Azami had come back to the past wanting to apologize and express gratitude based on that premise. *But what if she didn't?* Azami imagined Yumiko might hang up when she found out who was calling. Or worse – she might ask, 'Why are you calling now, after all this time?'

Her last exchange with Yumiko at the Tenmonkan Arcade flashed through her mind. She had violently shoved Yumiko – who was desperately trying to bring her home – saying, 'Just leave me be!'

From that day on, the smile had gradually faded from Yumiko's face.

Back then, I felt nothing, but now, just thinking about my mother's feelings brings me close to tears.

Azami's hands dropped to her lap. Her gaze wandered aimlessly.

I've been given such an opportunity to come back to the past, yet what am I doing? I never imagined I was this cowardly. After causing my mother so much distress, here I am, worrying about my feelings.

Azami was disappointed in her own selfishness, and felt like crying due to her pathetic inability to make the call.

At that moment . . .

'Who were you planning to call?' asked Kei, who had been watching her from behind the counter.

Azami looked up to see Kei's wide, round eyes staring right back at her.

'Hey, Kei,' Nagare said in a low voice, 'don't interfere.'

'But it's unusual, right? I've never heard of someone coming from the future just to make a phone call.'

In response to Kei's unfiltered observation, Nagare bowed to Azami in apology.

'Sorry.'

Oh, what am I doing?

Thanks to Kei and Nagare, Azami had come back to reality, and she realized that their act had been deliberate. Kei wasn't asking Azami out of curiosity about who she was calling – it was to remind her of the limited time available to her, a temporary visitor from the future. More evidence of such a ploy was how Kei was no longer smiling and instead sharing Nagare's look of concern as they watched her.

You can do it.

They conveyed their encouragement not by words but through their eyes, revealing a pureness, filled with prayer-like hope that her visit would not be in vain: that she would at least have heard the voice she was yearning for on the other end of the line before being returned to the future.

Azami was touched by their sentiment. She admired how sincerely supportive these two strangers were, despite having met her only minutes earlier. She always did her best to be kind to others, yet she acknowledged the difficulty of doing so to a stranger she had only recently met.

With a renewed frame of mind, she felt compelled to open up and share everything with these two. Staring at the handset, she told them who she was planning to call.

'My mother. I wanted to apologize to her . . . But then I thought how many years it had been without contact since I left home, and suddenly I had no idea what I would say to her.' She sighed.

This was her true feeling, which was akin to desperately wishing to confess, 'I love you,' to someone but not doing so because of fear – of not knowing how they feel about you, of being disliked or rejected.

'Why not just tell her you're doing well?' Kei suggested, tilting her head in her typically carefree and innocent way.

'Hey, hey,' chided Nagare, reacting to how Kei was offering advice while unaware of Azami's circumstances. Sensing from Azami's expression and demeanour that she might have had some trouble with her mother, Nagare gave Kei a reprimanding look.

Nevertheless, Kei continued unabated.

'If this is your last chance to speak with her, maybe just let her hear your voice? That might make her happy, don't you think?' she said, looking to Nagare for agreement.

He was caught off guard and stammered in response: 'Well, but that's just it, isn't it? Everyone has their own struggles, and we can't truly know whether her mother would be pleased, can we?'

Though he meant to empathize with and support Azami, 'everyone has their own struggles' struck a nerve.

I came here to apologize to my mother for my mistakes. It's a personal issue I alone need to resolve, and it's nothing to do with her. Even if what my father told me on the day of the funeral was a lie – he wouldn't have said it to hurt me, he would be saying it for his own reasons. Mum, too, has her own world. The possibility that my call would anger her was always on my mind. But I need to apologize – and that scares me. I'm afraid she won't forgive me. But that shouldn't stop me. I did something I need to apologize for, regardless of forgiveness. Now that I'm a stepmother like Mum, I came here to face my past and apologize.

Something settled in Azami's heart.

Let's do this!

Gazing at the handset with new-found resolve, Azami started pressing the buttons.

Kei beamed at Nagare. *Just as I said, right?*

Nagare in return let out a relieved sigh as if to say, *Well, either way, it's good. It would have been a shame if she returned to the future without doing anything.*

Even now resisting the urge to end the call, Azami slowly brought the receiver to her ear. Her heart was endlessly wavering between wanting the call to be answered and hoping it wouldn't be.

The ringtone, audible from the phone speaker, continued monotonously. Each time it repeated, Azami's heartbeat accelerated, making the wait feel interminable.

The ringtone stopped.

'Hello?'

Azami recognized the voice instantly. It was somewhat thinner than the voice of Yumiko in her memories. But she had no doubt that it was Yumiko who was speaking.

'Hello? Who is this?'

A tone of caution could be heard emerging in Yumiko's voice due to Azami's delay in responding.

'Er, um . . .'

Azami had intended to announce herself promptly. But, too fearful of how her stepmother might react, no words were forthcoming.

It's not too late to hang up. She still doesn't know it's me.

Her inner voice was coaxing her to lower the handset from her ear.

At that moment . . .

'Azami, is that you?'

From the handset now lowered from her ear, Azami could hear faintly the voice calling her name.

'Hello?' Azami whispered, wondering if she had misheard.

'Azami? Is it really you?'

'Yes,' Azami replied.

Her stepmother did not speak for several seconds.

On the phone it's impossible to know what the other person is thinking during such silences.

Azami wanted to say something, but she was so agitated, she couldn't muster anything at all.

'Er, um . . .'

'How have you been?'

Her stepmother's question caught her by surprise. It felt so out of the blue and yet so natural at the same time. Azami had left home without ever having had typical mother–daughter conversations, she had always called Yumiko 'you', and never 'Mum', it was a dozen or so years since they had lived under the same roof, and she had assumed that her stepmother had thought of her as more and more the stranger. Azami herself could not help but feel significant emotional distance between them, and so her stepmother's words prompted a rather distant-sounding response.

'I'm sorry for suddenly calling you like this . . .'

'Not at all. Certainly, don't apologize.'

Her stepmother's words sounded a little awkward, but they were kind. 'But I never thought you would call, so I also, um, don't know what to say . . .'

Her stepmother's words revealed her bewilderment. After Azami left home, there must have been a period when she hoped to hear from her. But Azami never called, not after three years, not after five. There must have come a time when she gave up expecting anything.

'I'm sorry.' This apology was all that Azami could offer.

Once again, silence. Azami guessed that her stepmother might also be perplexed, suddenly talking with her step-child who had not called for so long and was now only apologizing.

I've no business showing up in my mother's life now. It would only be fair that she's forgotten me. How would I feel if my daughter treated me the same way? It would be too painful to bear. My husband's daughter was kind, unlike me. She accepted me as her mother right away. Compared to her, how terrible was I? I can't regret it enough. How must my mother be feeling now? Apologizing to her won't change anything. The cafe's rules say, the present won't change. So my apology will bring about nothing for her.

Azami realized she wasn't getting the response she had hoped for.

I should go back.

She took a deep breath and started, 'Mum, I . . .'

She heard her stepmother's gasp. 'What?'

'Mum? What's up? Mum, did something happen? Are you OK?'

But there was no reply.

'Mum?'

Azami called out again, a bit louder this time.

When she pressed her ear firmly against the handset, she could hear the muffled sound of her stepmother sobbing. She must be covering her mouth as she cried.

Azami was unsettled by this as she could not understand why her stepmother would suddenly start crying.

'Mum, what's wrong? Are you OK?'

'I'm sorry, Azami.'

'Why are you apologizing? I'm the one at fault.'

'No, it's not that.'

'Not that? What then?'

'That made me so happy.'

'What did?'

'That was the first time you've ever called me "Mum", and it made me so happy.'

'Ah . . .'

Now that I'm older, I can see how my rebelliousness towards my mother has faded over the years. Sometimes I even wonder what I was so defiant about. It's almost startling, realizing that somewhere along the way, 'that woman' in my mind became simply . . . 'my mother'.

Azami had called Yumiko 'Mum' unconsciously. However, for Yumiko it was a word that must have struck her to the very core.

To think she would cry just from me calling her 'Mum'.

At that moment, Azami realized the depth of her stepmother's emotional wounds.

'I'm sorry, Mum. I'm really sorry. I have been hurting you for so long. I'm truly sorry for hurting you and not contacting you.'

Azami could not stop her tears either.

'It's OK, it's all right,' her stepmother replied, barely able to form the words.

For a while, silence fell over the two people connected over the phone. It was not a normal awkward silence, for even without words, their feelings had been clearly communicated to each other.

'Um . . .' Kei gently interrupted the moment, speaking to Azami, who could not stop crying. 'May I take the phone back now?' Kei was speaking close to the handset, as if to ensure Yumiko could hear on the other end.

Azami looked up at her, thinking, *There was no need to speak so loudly.* But when she looked into Kei's eyes, she saw the urgency. *The coffee is about to get cold.*

'Ah . . .'

Azami quickly came to her senses. She had travelled back in time. And there were rules.

CLANG-DONG

The doorbell rang suddenly. It was Nagare, who had been standing behind the counter.

'Hello, welcome, just for one, is it?' Kei asked him playfully. This odd interaction among the cafe's staff continued.

'Is that a cafe? Where are you speaking from?' Yumiko asked.

'Er, yes. I'm calling from a basement cafe.' Azami realized what Kei and Nagare had been doing – reminding her of her limited time and attempting to provide her an opportunity to end the call. 'I'm actually calling from a borrowed phone . . .'

'Oh, I see, sorry, sorry.'

'So . . .'

'Please call me again, OK? I'll be waiting.'

Azami was unsure how to respond. She would be lying if she made that promise. Once she returned to the present, her stepmother would be deceased. She would never be able to contact her again. But speaking honestly would only bring sadness. She hesitated only for a moment and answered as cheerfully as possible, trying not to betray her lie.

'Sure, of course.'

'Thanks for the call. Bye, then.'

Yumiko sounded reluctant yet soft and content.

'Mum . . .' Azami instinctively called out again. Kei and Nagare exchanged looks, worried about the coffee cooling down. Azami took the cup in her hand and brought it close to her lips. 'Thank you for loving me. I was a terrible daughter. But despite that, you kept loving me all this time, even till today.'

Having said that, Azami placed the handset on the table and quickly drank the coffee.

'Ah . . .'

Her vision blurred. Just as had happened on the journey there, her body transformed into white steam and then rose up and disappeared, as if sucked into the ceiling.

After confirming that Azami had safely returned to the future, Kei picked up the handset. Yumiko's sobs could be heard.

'That was something, wasn't it?' said Kei and she informed Yumiko that Azami had to leave the cafe in a hurry due to urgent business. Then, after hearing Yumiko's laboured breathing, she heard a man's voice. He introduced himself as

Azami's father. His last words were, 'Thank you very much. My wife says she has no regrets left now.'

Then he hung up.

January 2019

When Azami opened her eyes, she saw Fumiko sitting at the counter. Looking around the cafe, she saw that Kazu was there too. Kei and Nagare, who had lent her the phone, were nowhere to be seen.

I'm back.

Azami peered into the empty coffee cup she had finished drinking.

I must have drunk it just in time.

She remembered the chill she felt from the lukewarm coffee while gulping it down. Then, bringing her mind to the present, she realized her cheeks were wet and reached for a paper napkin on the table. Just then, the woman in the white dress returned from the restroom and loomed over Azami.

'Move!' she demanded.

Azami stood up hurriedly to relinquish her seat.

'It seems you were able to talk things through?' said Fumiko, approaching her.

'How do you know?'

'I can tell, just by looking at your face . . .'

'I see.'

Fumiko's words rang true. Indeed, the pain that had been a thorn at her heart was gone.

I must look relieved right now.

Without worrying about her ruined make-up, Azami smiled at Fumiko.

'I'm glad I could go back. Thank you.'

'I'm happy to hear that,' Fumiko replied, smiling in return.

Soon after, Azami said, 'I want to see my daughter's face,' and hurried out of the cafe.

CLANG-DONG

'Phew, I'm so relieved,' said Fumiko after accompanying Azami as far as street level to see her off. She sighed deeply – an expression of relief she hadn't shown in Azami's presence.

'Would you like something to drink?' asked Kazu as Fumiko settled onto a stool at the counter.

'Ah, I'll have a piping-hot coffee.'

'Coming right up.'

Fumiko watched Kazu disappear into the kitchen, then turned her gaze towards the woman in the white dress.

The more I look, the more they resemble each other . . .

Fumiko knew that the woman in the white dress was Kazu's mother. When Kazu was seven, she had poured the coffee that allowed her mother to travel back in time to see her father, who had passed away. But her mother never returned. Ever since hearing that story, Fumiko had been unable to shake a single question:

Why didn't Kazu's mother come back?

According to Nagare, Kazu's mother had been a bright, compassionate person who treated everyone with kindness.

She, of all people, would have known how critical it was to drink the coffee before it cooled if she wanted to return. After all, she had been the pourer of the coffee before Kazu.

For someone like that to leave her precious daughter and not come back, there must have been a serious reason. But Fumiko also understood that she wasn't close enough to Kazu to ask.

This is something I shouldn't bring up. After all, the person most hurt by all of this is Kazu, who was the one who poured the coffee for her mother.

While Fumiko was lost in thought, Kazu brought the coffee over. Instead of, 'Here's your coffee,' she said quietly, 'Back then, I thought my mother chose my father over me,' and she placed the cup in front of Fumiko.

'What?'

Fumiko froze. It was as if Kazu had just read her mind.

'But lately,' Kazu continued, ignoring Fumiko's surprise, 'I've started to wonder if there isn't really a hierarchy when it comes to how much we cherish someone. Maybe those feelings can't be compared.'

Then, looking at the woman in the white dress, she murmured, 'The fact that my mother never came back and the love she felt are two separate things . . .' It sounded as if she was reassuring herself.

Watching the unexpectedly tranquil look on Kazu's face,

Fumiko thought, *I've never seen her look so calm*, and felt a small surge of happiness.

Kazu returned to the other side of the counter and began polishing the cutlery as usual.

'Um . . .'

Fumiko leaned forward to watch Kazu's hands at work.

'Yes?' Kazu asked, pausing to look back at Fumiko.

'Mind if I help you with that?'

Kazu paused for a second before replying.

'Sure,' she said, and welcomed Fumiko behind the counter.

II

The Patient Man

Autumn 2012

Koku Shintani was gazing at one particular painting at his art college's cultural festival.

Titled *Mother*, the large canvas, 162 by 112 centimetres, depicted a railway crossing in the foreground, leading to a streetscape bathed in orange hues beyond. It was painted in a style known as hyperrealism, detailed enough to be mistaken for a photograph at first glance. So realistic, in fact, that if you didn't know it was a painting, it might even have appeared as if there was a rectangular hole in the wall.

On closer inspection, however, there was something odd about it. The scene included a bookshop, a bank, and a supermarket, with cars and bicycles moving through the street. But not a single person was visible. It wasn't a ghost town;

bags and backpacks were floating in mid-air, giving the eerie impression that everyone had turned invisible.

A shadow dominated the scene, stretching from the foreground to the background. Considering the title, *Mother*, one might assume the shadow to be that of a grown woman. Yet Koku, with his keen eyes, recognized the realistically drawn silhouette as belonging to a girl of around seven or eight years old.

Could it be that this girl is standing on . . .?

Koku was trying to deduce the girl's position from the composition of the painting. Judging by how the shadow was cast, she must have been standing on the tracks. As he looked at her shadow, he felt as if it was extending out from his own feet.

He swallowed hard. The realism and assurance of the painting were so intense that he half expected a train to appear from his side at any moment, and run him over. Gradually, the boundary between the painting and reality blurred even further, and he could even hear the clanging of the warning bell in his ears.

Koku was attending art college to become a photographer.

His interest in photography began when he was in elementary school, sparked by a hand-me-down DSLR camera he received from his father for his birthday. He took a liking to its heft and weight and, except when he was at school, he carried it everywhere. Initially, he indiscriminately captured anything that caught his eye. During summer and winter breaks, there were days he would take as many as a thousand or even two thousand photos.

By the time he reached junior high school, he had become more selective about his subjects, preferring to photograph old, abandoned houses and decayed, ancient trees.

When his father asked him, 'Do you really enjoy taking pictures of such things?'

Koku responded, 'Yes, I like capturing time.'

'Time? You can't capture time in a photograph, can you?'

Naturally, Koku's father was puzzled by this notion.

Koku had a unique sensibility; to him, the older the ruins or decayed trees, the more enchanting they appeared. By capturing these moments, seemingly on the verge of vanishing completely, he was preserving them for ever. That for him was the essence of photography. When he entered high school he began submitting his photographs to contests and occasionally won a prize. Around that time he also began to dream of travelling the world as a photographer.

He decided to attend an art university to study languages and the fundamentals of photography.

All of that led to him, now in his third year at university, encountering this painting.

Vividly depicting not only present-day reality but also the artist's inner emotions, the painting had a visceral impact on him, whose photos until then captured only remnants of the past that met his eye.

In that instant, he truly felt what it meant to have one's heart captured.

'Excuse me, we'll be closing shortly.'

A voice broke his reverie. It was a student he didn't recognize. Coming back to his senses, Koku realized that three hours had passed. Outside, darkness had fallen, and the lively campus had settled into silence.

'Who painted this?' Koku asked the student.

'Oh, er . . . who was it again?' The student, cooperating with a reluctant expression, glanced at the pamphlet on the reception desk of the exhibition room. 'It might be Kazu Tokita, a second-year student,' he answered noncommittally.

'Kazu Tokita.'

Koku repeated the name several times under his breath, then looked up at the painting again. Had he not been informed that it was closing time, he might have remained rooted to the spot indefinitely.

He felt an unprecedented surge of emotion and interest towards the artist Kazu Tokita.

Early spring 2019

The cafe Funiculi Funicula, rumoured to transport patrons back in time, was established in the year 1874, during the Meiji era. It was run by a woman named Toki Tokita. According to tradition, only the women of the Tokita family are allowed to pour the special coffee that enables time travel. Toki is reputed to have been the first owner of such a cafe in Japan; there are others scattered around the world. However, the origins of how the cafe was built and where Toki Tokita came from remain a mystery.

The current owner of the cafe was a man by the name of Nagare Tokita, who – always clad in his cook's uniform – stood nearly two metres tall.

Nagare's broad, understated face featured narrow, thread-like eyes and his build was sturdy, like a bodybuilder's. He was once hit by a runaway car, sent flying dozens of metres, yet walked away with nothing more than a few scratches – a feat that sounds more like a scene from a manga than real life.

He was a self-taught cook skilled in Japanese, Western, Chinese, and ethnic cuisines. He had received numerous offers from top-tier restaurants, but he consistently declined them even when offered a lucrative contract, saying, 'I have inherited this cafe and must continue to run it.' While most people associate cafes with light snacks, at Funiculi Funicula there was no dish that could not be served if requested. However, since these were not listed on the menu, the main orders from ordinary customers tended to be coffee and other drinks. The interior featured three two-seater tables and three counter seats. At the table furthest from the door, a woman in a white dress was always seated, and the rumour had it that her seat was the one that could take you back in time. Thus, there were only seven seats available for general customers. One reason the cafe never reached full capacity, though, was its inconspicuous location in an alleyway.

On this particular day, the only customers were a frequent

visitor, Fumiko Kiyokawa, and a young man named Koku Shintani.

'Koku, you appear to be quite the cameraman.'

Fumiko was sitting at the counter and flipping through a photo book.

'I think photographer is the correct term, right, Koku?'

Nagare was a stickler for precise wording, so he wasn't going to let Fumiko's misuse of terms pass. His brow was furrowed in reprimand.

'Well . . . yeah.'

Koku, sporting a casually styled spiral perm, shyly scratched his head.

'What's the difference?'

Fumiko asked the question in a flat voice, never lifting her gaze from the photo book.

'Er . . . Well . . .'

Though Nagare had insisted there was a distinction, he was unable to articulate it clearly. Narrowing his already thread-thin eyes, he fell silent. Fumiko looked up at him icily.

'They're basically two names for the same job,' Koku answered in a measured tone. 'But people who shoot video are also called cameramen, so I use the term photographer. I don't do video.'

His explanation was concise and easy to grasp. Some say that the most easily heard pitch in conversation is 'Sol' in the solfège scale (Do, Re, Mi, Fa, Sol, La, Ti). Koku's voice was exactly that – a gentle 'Sol' that gave a sense of comfort.

'I see.'

Fumiko had intended to scold Nagare for his know-it-all attitude, but she sensed Koku's tactful consideration towards him and let it slide. Instead, she shared her impression.

'But, Koku, even though your photos aren't videos, they somehow capture the passage of time – like if I look at the same page in three years, it might come across as something completely different. It's such a strange feeling.'

'Ah, yes! I've noticed that too,' Nagare said. 'It's like those dolls whose hair grows mysteriously. It reminds me of that.'

Fumiko scoffed at Nagare's comparison and looked at him disapprovingly.

'Seriously, Nagare, you couldn't come up with a better example? That's even ruder than mixing up photographer and cameraman.'

'What? Oh . . . I didn't mean anything strange by it . . .'

'I know. You're saying that the photos I take seem to be alive, right?'

'Yes . . . yeah, exactly.'

'I'm happy to hear that. Thank you,' Koku said, offering a gentle smile to Nagare, who was still visibly unnerved by Fumiko's comment. That single smile, radiating an unmistakable warmth and utterly free of pretence, seemed capable of forgiving anything.

Nagare's expression softened as he looked back at this younger man, a full eight years his junior.

'Likewise,' he replied with a small nod.

Observing their exchange, Fumiko sighed. *He's twenty-seven – one year older than Kazu. He's far too mature for his age.*

CLANG-DONG

As the doorbell rang, Nagare called out, 'Hello. Welcome!' The man stepping inside was Tomokazu Okishima, dressed youthfully in a beige spring coat and slim jeans.

'Oh,' Nagare said quietly on seeing his face.

'Afternoon,' Okishima said, nodding slightly. Removing his coat, he headed towards the vacant middle table.

From behind the counter, Nagare called out to Okishima, 'Is it that time of year already?'

'Yes, I'm back again,' Okishima replied.

Fumiko was a frequent visitor to the cafe, but today was the first time she had seen Okishima. She watched their exchange with a puzzled expression. Okishima hung his coat over the back of his chair and sat down facing away from the woman in the white dress.

Dong, dong.

One of the cafe's grand antique pendulum wall clocks had struck 2 p.m.

There were three pendulum wall clocks in the cafe, but only the one in the middle kept accurate time; the other two were either slow or fast. It was the middle clock that had rung out.

'Ah, then I'll be going now . . .' Prompted by the clock, Koku rose from his seat at the counter and reached for his carry-on case and the large backpack containing his camera equipment.

'Leaving already? Kazu should be back soon . . .' Nagare said, coming out from the kitchen to stop him.

'I have a flight to catch,' Koku explained. He placed the amount due on the counter and, with a heave, slung the heavy backpack onto his shoulders.

'Oh, and that is for Kazu,' Koku added, briefly glancing at the photo book open in front of Fumiko and then bowing to Nagare, who responded with an OK sign.

'Ah . . . yes, of course.' Only at that moment did Fumiko realize the photo book Koku had brought with him had been for Kazu. Looking a little flustered, she carefully closed its pages and set it on the counter.

'The coffee was delicious as always.'

'Take care,' Nagare called after him as Koku pulled his carry-on case behind him and left the cafe.

CLANG-DONG

After seeing Koku off, Nagare served water to Okishima, who didn't even glance at the menu before ordering.

'I'll have a coffee and the pasta of the day, please.'

'Certainly,' responded Nagare, his eyes briefly sparking with excitement – a chance to showcase his culinary skills always delighted him. He hurried into the kitchen.

At the counter, Fumiko reopened the photo book. After

flipping through a few pages and taking in the images, she called to Nagare.

'Is he, by any chance, dating Kazu?' she asked.

'Are you talking about Koku?' Nagare replied, peeking out from the kitchen.

'He seems like a nice person,' Fumiko remarked.

She had long sensed that Koku had feelings for Kazu, but after four years of visiting the cafe she had convinced herself that Kazu simply wasn't the type to get involved in a relationship.

Kazu always seemed to keep people at arm's length, avoiding any deeper connection. Over those same four years, Fumiko had reached the point of exchanging jokes and playful banter with Nagare, yet she still sensed a significant wall when it came to Kazu. Naturally, this made Fumiko all the more curious about how Kazu felt about Koku.

However, Nagare's response to Fumiko's question was as ambiguous as she had expected.

'Hard to say, really.'

Nagare and Kazu were cousins. Nagare was gentle at heart, and as a chef, showed meticulous care in his work. Yet when it came to things he found uninteresting – especially romance – he simply couldn't care less. He had met his wife Kei when he was hospitalized after a traffic accident. She proposed to him so fervently, he accepted almost as casually as if he was being asked out for a walk. He was the first to admit that had Kei not come along, he might have stayed single all his life. Even three years after her death, he had not considered remarrying.

Given this background, it was no surprise that he couldn't provide any insights into Kazu and Koku's relationship.

I was foolish to enquire, thought Fumiko, sighing again as she watched Nagare carry coffee to Okishima.

CLANG-DONG

As the clang of the doorbell reached everyone's ears, a cheerful voice echoed from the entrance.

'I'm back!'

Nagare's face tightened as he served coffee to Okishima.

The newcomer was Miki Tokita, the daughter of Nagare and Kei. At barely three years old, she was the very picture of an outgoing and carefree personality – something she inherited from her mother. Without any shyness, she would talk to anyone.

'The cherry blossoms haven't come yet.'

Miki sat on Nagare's foot and wrapped her arms and legs around his shin, clinging to him. This was her recently favoured game, and Nagare would move around with her perched on his foot.

She continued, saying, 'Daddy's walking for me,' and showed no signs of letting go.

After a while, Kazu appeared from behind Miki. Nagare, with a sigh mingled in his whisper, said, 'Thanks for letting Miki get her way. It was nice of you to take her out.'

'No problem,' Kazu replied nonchalantly.

As Nagare walked carefully into the kitchen with Miki still perched on his foot, Fumiko commented to Kazu, 'It seems it was still a bit early for cherry blossom viewing.'

'Yes,' Kazu responded curtly, but Fumiko wasn't deterred and continued the conversation.

'I love it the most when the cherry blossoms start to fall. Watching the petals flutter down, you can lose track of time,' she said.

'That's true,' Kazu replied.

'There's fleeting beauty, but it also stirs up literary images. For me, my mind wanders to Hideki Noda's stage adaptation of Ango Sakaguchi's *In the Forest, Under Cherries in Full Bloom*. His last scene was just wow. There was a massive blizzard of cherry blossoms swirling around the performers – Noda played a man with huge ears – it was epic, humans intermingling with demons . . .'

While Fumiko excitedly talked about cherry blossoms and theatre, Kazu took off her navy-blue duffel coat, went into the back room and returned wearing a sommelier's apron.

'After seeing that, I really got into theatre. Do you ever go to see plays, Kazu?'

'No.'

'Let's go together. There's an interesting play coming up next month.'

'I . . .'

'Come on, don't be like that, let's do it!'

Fumiko quickly overlaid her words, not giving Kazu much room to refuse.

Kazu was silent for a moment as she tied her apron strings. 'OK,' she finally said, a response that seemed neither eager nor reluctant. It sounded like she agreed simply because she found no reason to decline.

'Great!' Fumiko clapped her hands with excitement as if she had won the lottery.

'Oh, he dropped by?' Kazu's gaze fell on the photo book that Koku had brought.

'Yes, he was here just a while ago. But he had a flight . . .'

Fumiko, showing a hint of regret for not mentioning Koku's visit earlier amidst their talk of cherry blossoms and theatre, handed the book to Kazu, hoping for a reaction, but . . .

'Oh, I see,' said Kazu blandly, her expression unchanged. She took the book into the back, where living spaces for her and Nagare were annexed to the cafe. Fumiko couldn't tell whether she was pleased with the book or found it a nuisance.

Nor could she fathom from Kazu's usual detached and impassive demeanour what she might be feeling about the affection Koku likely harboured for her.

'Hmm.'

'What is it? Is something wrong?' Nagare, emerging from the kitchen, tilted his head inquisitively.

On one arm was a tray bearing the pasta Okishima had ordered, and in the other was Miki. Three-year-old Miki, cradled by the nearly two-metre-tall Nagare, resembled a small animal, momentarily capturing Fumiko's attention with its sweetness.

'Oh, no, it's nothing,' she replied quickly, waving her hand dismissively and reaching for her half-finished iced coffee.

Just then, as if on cue, Kazu returned. With merely a glance, she took the tray from Nagare and approached Okishima's table.

Nagare waited for the moment Kazu placed the dish in front of him, then explained, 'I had a can of mackerel in miso, so I mixed it with tomato sauce and added plenty of garlic, along with some red chilli peppers, salt, and pepper to season it. Feel free to add these to taste,' he said as he set down some grated cheese and Tabasco next to the dish.

'Thank you,' Okishima responded, his eyes sparkling as he looked at the pasta and picked up his fork.

'It smells good,' Fumiko remarked from her seat at the counter, taking a deep breath.

'Ah, sorry about that,' Okishima paused, noticing Fumiko's envious gaze.

'No, no! Please, don't mind me, go ahead and enjoy your meal!' Fumiko quickly regretted making Okishima, whom she had just met, feel self-conscious, and she bowed her head and hunched her shoulders.

Okishima also apologized for making Fumiko feel uncomfortable, and then he clasped his hands together, saying, 'Well then, excuse me,' before he began twirling the pasta on his fork. The mackerel had been well flaked and melded beautifully with the tomato sauce, which clung to the pasta.

'Delicious,' Okishima murmured appreciatively.

Nagare narrowed his thin eyes even further, a sign that he took great pleasure in watching his customers enjoy the dishes he prepared.

'That's odd. What happened to Miki?' Fumiko noticed something unusual about Miki, who was typically non-stop chatty even when Nagare was busy working. Now, she was unusually quiet.

'Did she fall asleep?'

'It seems so,' Nagare replied.

Breathing softly, snuggled up in Nagare's arms, Miki was sound asleep. Even without the cherry blossoms, it was easy to imagine her running around in the park until she was completely worn out. Nagare sighed with resignation.

'How cute,' Fumiko murmured.

'Sorry, can you take over the shop for a bit?'

'Of course.'

Nagare, trusting Kazu with the cafe, took Miki into the back room to put her to bed.

With Nagare and Miki gone, the cafe was eerily quiet. Since no music played, the only sound was Okishima twirling his pasta with his fork. Kazu was naturally reticent, and Fumiko and Okishima were meeting for the first time.

Okishima tried to think of something suitable to talk about, but overwhelmed by Fumiko's appearance, he couldn't find an opening. Fumiko's features aligned perfectly with the classical concept of the Golden Ratio, marking ideal proportions and placement of eyes, nose, and mouth. Her face was small, with sharp, well-defined features, and she had clear skin with glossy lips. Her black hair, tied back, was full and lustrous, with curly tips bouncing attractively. Okishima felt intimidated and, worried that any attempt to strike up a conversation might be misinterpreted as flirting, shrank into his shell.

Fumiko, her head tilted in curiosity, suddenly leaned in to ask Okishima, 'Did you come here to go back in time?'

Given that the cafe was rumoured to have a seat that could transport people back in time, and considering Fumiko herself had experienced such a journey four years ago, it seemed to her a natural question. In fact, she found it unusual for someone to visit the cafe for any other reason.

'Ah, um,' Okishima stammered. In the dim windowless cafe, Fumiko's eyes sparkled so brightly that they seemed to give off their own light, and he was too flustered to grasp her question.

'Did you come here because of the rumours about this cafe?' Fumiko pressed on, undeterred.

'Rumours? Oh, yes!'

Okishima finally nodded in understanding, a bit too vigorously, almost dropping his fork and accidentally kicking the table, nearly tipping over a glass of water.

'Are you OK?' Fumiko stood up, concerned.

'Yes, I'm fine. Sorry about that.' Okishima raised his hand to stop her from coming closer. After placing his fork down and making sure the water hadn't spilled, he reassured her again, 'It's OK,' and waited for Fumiko to sit again.

'I'm actually waiting for someone,' he admitted.

'You have arranged to meet them?' Fumiko enquired.

'Yes, well.' Okishima's face clouded slightly. Fumiko didn't miss the change in his expression and instinctively looked back at Kazu, wondering if she might know the reason. Her intuition was right.

'Mr Okishima has travelled back in time before.'

'What?' Fumiko spun her head round to Kazu. The way Okishima had avoided eye contact with Kazu as he said, *Yes, well*, now made sense. Kazu had indeed known more of the story.

From the casual familiarity Okishima shared with Nagare, Fumiko inferred that he had visited the cafe several times before. He surely knew precisely which seat enabled time travel. Yet he chose a seat facing away from the woman in the white dress, indicating that he hadn't come for that on this occasion.

Fumiko's curiosity shifted subtly – from wondering if Okishima came to travel back in time to questioning who he might be waiting for, given he had already made that journey. Her gaze lingered thoughtfully on him. With this new insight, she seemed to brim with unspoken questions.

Picking up on her inquisitive stare, Okishima calmly lifted a paper napkin, wiping a stray splash of tomato sauce from the table, and began softly.

'I went back in time seven years ago.'

14 February 2012

Okishima, a junior-high second-grader, was restless and distracted, unable to focus on his lessons. He was not alone. All the boys in Class 8-D were visibly anxious, glancing around and reacting to the movements of the girls during breaks.

The reason? It was Valentine's Day.

In Japan, Valentine's Day has evolved into an occasion when women express their affection to men by giving chocolates. Even girls who are usually too shy to confess find the courage to do so on this day, spurred by the noble excuse of Valentine's Day. As a result, each year after the 14th of February, new couples invariably form in the class.

Puberty typically begins between the ages of ten and fourteen. Boys' bodies start to fill out, and facial hair begins to appear. Boys who were shorter than the girls in elementary school may shoot up, their frames becoming noticeably more 'boyish'. Around this time, the classmates and friends they used to play with so innocently start to be seen in a different light – members of the opposite sex, and sometimes the same sex.

Okishima was no exception. As his mind and body began to change, he started seeing girls in a new way. In elementary school he didn't care a bit about untidy hair, but once he reached junior high he fussed over his hairstyle constantly. During every break, he'd sneak off to the bathroom to check his hair in the mirror – all for the sake of impressing the girls. But despite wanting to be popular, Okishima, who was shy by nature and stubborn in his own way, couldn't bring himself to simply join the girls' circle. When he saw one or two good-looking boys in class getting all the attention from the girls, he'd scoff, 'Show-offs,' spitting the words out with thinly veiled resentment.

Of course he was jealous. He wanted to be doted on, too. He just couldn't admit it. So instead, without even realizing it, he found a kind of comfort in pretending he didn't care – that girls simply didn't interest him. But even Okishima, as it turned out, had a girl he couldn't help but notice.

Her name was Kanna Ozaki. She had fair skin and the poised, delicate features of a traditional china doll. She was a head taller than most girls in her year group and was a good fit for her chosen sport of volleyball, although she didn't particularly stand out in her team. Contrary to the sport's frenetic nature, she was soft-spoken and rarely said a word.

Okishima and Kanna were classmates in the first year of junior high. What made him start noticing her was something his friend Shigeki Hayashida said, with a teasing grin: 'Kanna's always looking at you.'

From that moment on, he couldn't help but see her a little differently. Of course, it was impossible to say whether or not Hayashida's comment was true. Maybe he had feelings for Kanna himself, and when he was watching her, Okishima had simply been in her line of sight. People tend to return affection when they feel it from someone else – a tendency known as 'reciprocal liking'. Even if Kanna hadn't actually been looking at him, it was still true that Hayashida had said those words. Whether to believe it or not, that was up to Okishima. In the end, for better or worse, he believed it.

Once he started noticing Kanna, it felt like she was always looking his way. Their eyes met often – and by that point, whether Hayashida had been right didn't matter any more.

Okishima had fallen for Kanna, completely. But that didn't mean he planned to confess. After all, in his mind, *she* had liked *him* first – of that, he was absolutely certain.

Okishima, shy and contrary. Kanna, quiet and reserved.

At the start of the second term, a random seat shuffle placed them side by side.

But even sitting that close, the only words they ever exchanged throughout the day were hello and goodbye.

'Good morning.'

'Er . . . hey.'

'See you.'

'Y-yeah.'

And that was it – just two classmates.

Time passed, and in the second grade Okishima and Kanna were in different classes. Still, whenever they met, Kanna always greeted him, just like before. Then came Valentine's Day – an opportunity to turn their relationship into something else.

On that day, Okishima was hopeful that Kanna would give him chocolate. During the break periods he drifted past her classroom, sneaking a look inside to see if she was there.

Even after the first and second periods, Kanna was nowhere to be seen. When Okishima returned to his classroom, he saw a few boys being handed chocolates.

The boys who usually hung out with Okishima said,

'What's the big deal?;

'I'm not even into sweets.'

Whether they were truly annoyed or just saving face, who could say?

'Yeah, totally,' Okishima said, nodding along – though deep down, he was still hoping Kanna might give him chocolate. In reality, he didn't agree with the others at all.

Hayashida – the one who'd told him, 'Ozaki's always looking at you' – was in the group too. But after that, he'd started making little comments that hinted he might be interested in her himself. 'You know,' he said once, 'when you really look at her, she's actually kind of cute.'

'She's in Class 2-B?' Okishima posed a question. Of course, he knew that, but he was feigning ignorance.

'Yeah, yeah.'

'If we're talking about girls from 2-B, I think Izumi is prettier.'

Okishima named someone else on purpose – anything to keep Hayashida from realizing he liked Kanna.

'You might want to give up on Izumi.'

'Why?'

'Because . . .' Hayashida's eyes darted warily left and right, then he leaned in and whispered so only Okishima could hear. 'I heard she's dating Matsushita.'

Like Hayashida, Matsushita had been Okishima's classmate since elementary school. They weren't especially close, but Matsushita had always been popular with the girls, which was something Okishima had long resented.

'What?'

He didn't even like Izumi, but the thought of her going out with Matsushita filled him with irritation. Irritation, jealousy – and frustration. Matsushita had always been fawned over, and in the end, it seemed that the girls always went for the good-looking boys.

If Okishima *had* liked Izumi, the shock might've been enough to make him skip school for two or three days. But Kanna was the one he had real feelings for.

'Seriously . . .'

'Tough break,' Hayashida said, slinging an arm around Okishima. But he didn't exactly look as if he meant it.

His face practically glowed with smug satisfaction at being privy to a secret that Okishima hadn't heard, like he was savouring the sweetness of someone else's misfortune. Still, as far as Okishima was concerned, Kanna liked him back. The more words of comfort Hayashida offered, relishing his own imagined superiority, the more pathetic he seemed. That was why Okishima really didn't want to get chocolate in front of Hayashida. If Kanna handed it to him with Hayashida watching, he wouldn't know what kind of face to make – and, honestly, he felt bad for him.

He did feel sorry for him – but there's nothing uglier than pity from the winner to the loser. During breaks, Okishima did his best to slip out of the classroom and stay away from Hayashida.

In the few minutes between the third and fourth periods, he once again checked in on Class 2-B, pretending he was on his way to the toilet, but Kanna was nowhere in sight.

Is she avoiding me?

That dark thought came out of nowhere. Maybe he'd just got his hopes up too high, because now he couldn't shake the anxiety creeping in.

What if Ozaki likes Hayashida rather than me? That would be the worst.

From there, his thoughts spiralled into darker realms.

What if Hayashida confessed without me knowing? What if she used to like me, but now . . . she's falling for him?

Hayashida's weirdly smug expression from that conversation about Matsushita and Izumi suddenly flashed into his mind.

Wait – is Hayashida already dating Ozaki? Did he know I liked her, and say all that on purpose? If that's true . . .

As he walked past Class 2-B, Okishima turned around suddenly, heart thudding. Was Hayashida watching him from somewhere?

'Maybe I'm overthinking this,' he muttered to himself.

Is she off school today?

That seemed the most likely explanation. If she was at home ill on Valentine's Day, that would explain not running into her. It wasn't impossible.

Come to think of it, she's missed school events and field trips before.

Of course, it had to be *today*, of all days. That part was frustrating. But still – it wasn't nearly as painful as the idea of seeing her give chocolate to Hayashida. Okishima let out a long sigh.

DING-DONG DANG-GONG

The bell for fourth period echoed through the school. *I guess Kanna really is off school today*, Okishima told himself as he headed back to class.

In the end, he didn't see her: not once, all day. He wasn't in any clubs so he usually went straight home after school, but that day he stayed in the classroom with Hayashida and a few other boys, chatting about nothing in particular.

None of them had got any chocolate – at least, not the kind that you give to someone you really like. Okishima and Hayashida had picked up two or three of the polite kind passed out by nice girls to every boy in the room.

As the hour passed four in the afternoon, the sun, low on the horizon, cast a warm orange glow across the classroom. The dismissal announcement came over the PA system. Cheers from the soccer and baseball teams stopped suddenly, leaving silence. The boys were finally starting to give up on what was really keeping them there. 'Want to head off?' someone muttered. A few sighed in resignation, and everyone reached for their bags.

But Okishima couldn't stand up. Thinking about how he'd spent the whole day full of hope just made him feel pathetic. Maybe Kanna didn't feel the same way – and saw him no differently from the rest of the boys who had stayed back?

One by one, his friends started heading for the door. Okishima overcame his reluctance to move and forced himself to stand.

Just then, the door rattled open. Hayashida, who was reaching for the handle, jumped back as it slid open on its own.

Their classmate Misuzu Horie was standing in the doorway. The boys who'd stuck around hoping for real Valentine chocolate tensed up. Getting some now would be like hitting a walk-off grand slam.

Misuzu gave them an exasperated look. 'You guys still here?'

'So what? It's no big deal,' Hayashida shot back. 'What about you? Why'd you come back – forget something?' His voice rose slightly, betraying a touch of excitement he couldn't quite hide.

Judging by Misuzu's attitude, there was little chance she'd brought chocolate. Still, just getting to talk to a girl when he thought he'd be heading home alone made Hayashida quietly happy. But that froze in an instant.

Misuzu, her hand still on the door, glanced at Hayashida and said, 'That's not it.' Then she looked at Okishima. Hayashida followed her gaze.

'Okishima, got a minute?'

She jerked her chin towards the hallway.

'Huh?' all the boys – including Okishima – blurted out.

'Just come here, will you?'

'Er – yeah.' Okishima, trying not to look flustered, started walking over. The other boys held back their envy, forcing awkward smiles.

He weaved through them towards the doorway, his emotions a swirl of guilt, confusion, and just a hint of excitement. All day, he'd been hoping to see Kanna – maybe even get chocolate from her – but she hadn't shown up. He'd even started to wonder if she was avoiding him. And now, just as the day was ending, a different girl had called his name. His heart fluttered. And, yeah – it felt kind of good to be the only one who got called out.

Okishima followed Misuzu out into the hallway, feeling light on his feet – until his heart nearly leapt from his chest. There, just beyond the classroom's view and only a few steps away, stood Kanna.

She stood with her hands behind her back, head down, looking shy.

'Ozaki . . .?' The word, barely a whisper, was uttered by Hayashida behind him.

'Ozaki's always looking at you.'

'You know . . . when you really look at her, she's actually kind of cute.'

Hayashida's words echoed vividly in Okishima's mind.

'Kanna's got something she wants to give you,' Misuzu said, arms crossed, planting herself between them. From her voice alone, it was obvious she'd had enough of Kanna's hesitation – and had dragged her here whether Kanna liked it or not.

Maybe she'd spent the whole day torn between giving him the chocolate or not. And the way Misuzu looked at him said it all, as if she was wondering, *What on earth does she see in this boy?* But right now, Okishima was too focused on Kanna – on what she might do next – to care.

But Kanna didn't move.

'It is time to go home. All students still remaining, please leave promptly.'

The PA system had cut through the brief silence once again. Only Misuzu – still playing go-between – looked up in response and sighed.

'We're out of time,' she said to Kanna.

'Yeah.' Kanna reached behind her back and brought out a small paper bag she'd been hiding. 'Here.'

Her voice was barely more than a whisper, and in her hand the paper bag was trembling. It was matt red with 'HAPPY VALENTINE' stamped in gold – a clear indication that it was not meant for just anyone.

This was chocolate from the heart, a real confession, from Kanna to Okishima. And thanks to Misuzu's total lack of subtlety, it was all happening in front of several other boys.

'Wait – for me?'

'Obviously! What are you saying? Just take it.'

That wasn't Kanna. It was Misuzu, sounding thoroughly annoyed.

'Ah, ah, right,' Okishima muttered, eyes still cast down as

he reached out with his right hand. His heart was pounding. Embarrassment made him clumsy, but somehow, he managed to take the chocolate. He was happy – of course he was – but he couldn't help feeling a little guilty for how excited he'd got earlier when Misuzu had called him.

Still, that didn't matter now. There was something he needed to do.

First, he had to get those words out of his mouth and say, 'Thank you.' Because from today onwards, they really liked each other – for real.

He tried to smile and get the words out, even if his nerves made it a little stiff.

'But, Okishima – don't you like Izumi?'

The hallway, glowing orange from the setting sun, froze – as if all its colour had suddenly drained away. In that moment, Okishima didn't even realize who had said it.

'What the hell is that supposed to mean?' Misuzu fired back.

She'd already handed things off with a sharp 'Whatever, work it out yourselves' and was about to head home when the comment landed.

'I, er . . . heard earlier that Okishima likes Izumi.'

That's when Okishima finally realized – the voice that froze the air belonged to Hayashida.

'Seriously? Now?'

Misuzu said exactly what Okishima was thinking.

'Wait, I just . . .'

When Okishima turned around, Hayashida looked like he didn't even know why he'd said it.

'Sorry.'

'I'm sorry.'

The words came from both sides – Kanna in front, Hayashida behind – spoken at the same time. And just like that, both of them turned and ran, as if they couldn't get away fast enough.

'Kanna!' Misuzu called out, and chased after her.

The boys who had been joking around moments earlier just slipped away, not even saying goodbye.

Early spring 2019

'What?!' Fumiko cried out, her voice echoing through the cafe as she listened to Okishima's story.

Okishima's eyes widened in surprise. He stared at Fumiko as she sprang up from her seat at the counter, a hand pressed to her mouth. But he was the only one who seemed startled. Behind the counter, Kazu stood unbothered, as if nothing had happened, while the woman in the white dress sat quietly, reading her book.

'S-sorry,' Fumiko muttered, her face flushed.

'No, no,' Okishima replied, as she sat back down in her seat at the counter, still covering her face with both hands.

'And then? What happened next?' she asked, still feeling a little bad for her outburst – but even more curious to hear the rest of the story.

'That day, I was too shaken up to do a thing,' he said quietly.

'You didn't go after them? It was clearly just a misunderstanding, wasn't it?' she pressed.

He lowered his gaze and sighed as if the life had gone out of him. 'Yes . . . that's true, but . . . I just thought it'd make me look pathetic – trying to explain myself,' he confessed.

'But . . .' she began, then bit back the words, thinking, *If you'd just explained things properly, they would've understood.* It was seven years ago. There was no point in saying it now – and besides, he already knew that himself.

'And, I felt guilty, too. I had feelings for Ozaki, but the moment Horie called my name, she just – vanished from my mind. And I thought . . . *Was that really all my feelings for her amounted to?*'

Okishima laughed drily. His eyes were fixed on the cold pasta in front of him.

'If I'd really meant to accept chocolate from Ozaki and no one else . . . maybe I would've run after her.'

Fumiko found herself liking Okishima for his honesty. It was an admirable strength. But at the same time it was his weakness. He was incapable of pretending, even about his feelings.

No one could have known about the faint stir of emotion he felt in that brief moment between Misuzu calling his name and his first step into the hallway. He could've just kept quiet. But he couldn't forgive himself – he couldn't accept even that fleeting impurity in his heart.

Fumiko wondered, *What would I have done?* Then she knew:

she would have run after the person, even if, like Okishima, she'd wavered for a moment.

If a moment of doubt meant losing someone important to me, I'd bury it deep and never tell a soul – not for the rest of my life.

That was how Fumiko thought. That was simply who she was.

Even so, it wasn't as if she couldn't understand how Okishima had felt. She knew someone with a personality much like his: Goro Katada, her fiancé. And those qualities were exactly what made him so endearing to her.

She couldn't bring herself to say anything to Okishima. She believed that someone, someday, would see the charm in his simple honesty and emotional clumsiness.

She only murmured, almost to herself, 'I think I understand.'

'Would you like it reheated?' Kazu asked, breaking the silence. Her suggestion was partly spurred by Okishima staring at his cold pasta and, typically for her, partly in consideration that it might disappoint Nagare to see his food left uneaten.

'Ah, yes please,' Okishima said, his face lighting up. He would have eaten it cold – he didn't want to leave any. But he might as well enjoy it warm. Kazu took the plate back into the kitchen.

Fumiko, watching Kazu's retreating figure, suddenly tilted her head in thought.

If this is where his story ends, who exactly did he go back in time to meet?

Okishima had mentioned that he had travelled back to the past seven years ago. From the flow of the conversation, it was clear he had gone to see Kanna. So why was he still coming to the cafe?

No, that's not all of it, Fumiko's intuition protested.

There had to be a significant reason why he came to this cafe, sat with his back to the woman in the white dress, and occasionally stared intently at the entrance. Fumiko was convinced of it.

As her thoughts wandered, the sound of the microwave finishing echoed from the kitchen. Given that the aftermath of Valentine's Day had led to what seemed like an irretrievable blunder in Okishima's life, the comical 'ding' added an ironic touch to the moment. Perhaps sensing the same absurdity, Okishima met Fumiko's gaze and burst into laughter.

'Sorry to keep you waiting,' said Kazu, unaware of the reason for their laughter, as she returned with the tray bearing the reheated pasta. 'Here you go.'

'Thank you,' Okishima responded, bowing his head slightly to hide his amusement about the microwave from Kazu.

'Take your time,' she said with her usual composed demeanour as she returned behind the counter.

Determined not to let the pasta cool down again, Okishima finished his plate.

'By the way, who are you waiting for?' Fumiko asked, timing her question just as Okishima laid his cutlery neatly on his scraped-clean plate and let out a satisfied sigh. She was the kind of person who couldn't rest until she got an answer. Naturally, she expected him to say 'Kanna Ozaki'. But what she really wanted to hear about was everything that had happened since that Valentine's Day seven years ago.

'Of course, Kanna Ozaki,' Okishima replied, his gaze drifting towards the entrance. His response was as Fumiko anticipated, yet it left her feeling unsatisfied. There was a shadow in his expression when he said he was waiting for Kanna – a weariness, almost. Not the fatigue of a long day, but something deeper – the quiet exhaustion that builds over seven years of waiting.

Now that she thought about it, when Okishima came in, Nagare had said, 'Is it that time of year already?'

It suggested that Okishima came to the cafe every year around this time – or maybe on a fixed date – and each time, he waited for Kanna.

Judging by his expression, Fumiko suspected that Okishima still hadn't seen her, not even once. And yet something didn't sit right.

Why this time of year? Why keep waiting – for seven long years? Something essential was missing: why had Okishima gone back to the past?

'Why did you go back, seven years ago?' Fumiko asked, cutting straight to the point.

The wooden ceiling fan spun slowly over Okishima's head, as if rewinding time for him.

'Actually . . .' he began, his voice trailing off into the cafe's quiet hum. Slowly, he started to speak about what had happened that day.

14 February 2012

'Hey, how long are you planning to hang around? Go home!'

As twilight crept in Okishima was standing alone in the hallway. He was jolted back to himself by a teacher's distant shout. The paper bag Kanna had given him hung from his hand. It had only happened a few minutes ago, yet he couldn't clearly remember what had taken place. No – that wasn't it. He just couldn't accept it.

It wasn't until he got home that he realized he'd left his school bag behind. His wallet was in it, but that was the last thing on his mind. All he could think about was what had happened in that hallway, and how to set things right. In the bag Kanna had given him was a box shaped like a fairy-tale treasure chest, with a card nestled beside it.

Her message was in dainty pink handwriting.

If you don't like it, feel free to throw it away – Ozaki

He opened the box to find seven bite-sized treats – biscuits sandwiching marshmallows, each coated in chocolate.

'Like I could ever throw this away,' Okishima muttered with a bitter expression, placing the little treasure chest back into the paper bag.

Not until I've cleared things up.

He glanced at the clock. It was already past 7 p.m.

He wanted to talk to Kanna as soon as possible, but he didn't even have her number. He thought about asking one of the girls from their old class who might know how to reach her, but he hadn't exchanged contact info with any of them. Of the boys in his contacts, only Matsushita came to mind as someone who might know, but honestly, if Matsushita *did* have her number, that didn't sit right with him either.

But then Okishima thought that even if he managed to get her number, could he really bring himself to call her? They'd barely even exchanged more than a simple hello at school. Now he was supposed to just call and explain everything that had happened in the hallway?

Yeah . . . calling's not going to work.

He paced back and forth in his tiny room.

What should I do?

Even if he showed up at Kanna's home now, what would he say if her parents asked, 'So . . . what's going on between you and Kanna?' Just the thought made his heart lurch.

His thoughts kept spinning, going nowhere, and before he knew it, the clock had crept past 10 p.m.

I'll have to talk to her at school.

It was only then that he realized he was still wearing his school uniform.

His phone buzzed – it was a message. While pulling off his uniform, he stared at the phone. No one sent him messages this late.

Could it be?

He knew it was probably impossible, but still – his heart raced. Maybe it was from Kanna.

He reached for the phone, hesitantly. Hayashida's name lit up on the screen.

'What?'

Just like that, the excitement in his chest turned to irritation.

He'd been doing his best not to think about Hayashida. He was irritated, sure – but the truth was, he'd said, 'Izumi is prettier,' right to Hayashida's face. And obviously, Hayashida didn't have to tell everyone at that moment – right when Kanna had handed him the chocolate – but if he really did have feelings for her . . . Okishima couldn't bring himself to completely hate him.

Right now, the last thing he wanted was to even think about him, let alone read what he texted. Okishima flung his phone and uniform aside and slipped under the covers.

But sleep eluded him. 4 a.m. came round and he was still wide awake, wondering how to get a moment alone with Kanna at school. Approach her during break and call her out in front of everyone? No way – that kind of embarrassment would kill him. In the end, he decided the best option was to wait for her after school, by the front gate.

Still, he had his doubts.

Will she even believe me?

He knew full well how bad he was at talking. If he didn't

write it all out first, he'd probably just end up rambling and confuse her even more.

I shouldn't have told that stupid lie . . .

The best thing to do is just be honest about everything. Lame lies only make things worse. So, I'll just come out and say it – I like you!

With that decision made, he finally fell asleep.

The shrill sound of the alarm clock jolted Okishima awake. The February morning chill made his room feel like a freezer and his warm breath billowed into white mist.

He remembered the day's big mission. *All right!* He slapped his cheeks with both hands to pump himself up. This was probably going to be the day that took the most courage in all his fourteen years.

DING-DONG DANG-DONG

Okishima dashed into the classroom just as the starting bell rang. He was almost late after forgetting he'd left his bag at school and tearing through the house looking for it. But on the bright side, that meant he didn't have to run into Hayashida first thing and deal with that weird tension.

Their desks were in opposite corners of the classroom, Okishima's near the front by the windows, and Hayashida's at the back by the hallway. As long as he didn't turn round, he wouldn't have to see him.

Whenever Hayashida left his seat during breaks, Okishima

slipped out of the classroom to avoid him, then delayed his return to just before classes resumed, continuing to keep his distance. If Hayashida apologized now, he wouldn't even know how to react.

I just want to make it to the end of the day without seeing his face.

Throughout the morning, he occasionally felt Hayashida's gaze on him but made a conscious effort to not even turn his head towards the hallway. He couldn't focus on the lessons at all.

When fourth period ended and lunch break began, he dashed out of his classroom then hurried past Kanna's. He couldn't meet her just yet. He'd decided before falling asleep that confessing his feelings would have to wait until after school, when they could be alone. The last thing he wanted was to meet her surrounded by other students and just end up standing there in awkward silence.

But as he passed Kanna's classroom he sensed something was off.

He stopped and looked inside. No one was smiling. Heads were down, and they ate in silence.

It's like someone died.

He shrugged uncomfortably and kept walking.

'Okishima,' a familiar voice called from behind him. Something about it stopped him in his tracks. He turned around to see Misuzu, who'd been there when it all went down yesterday, standing with a serious look.

Oh no. He followed his first instinct – to walk away.

'Wait!'

Misuzu remained silent for a moment before finally whispering, '. . . was in an accident.'

'What?' Okishima couldn't quite catch her words, but an unsettling premonition washed over him, and he felt his heartbeat quicken with anxiety. 'Who did you say?'

'Kanna.'

'What?'

'Yesterday, Kanna was in an accident.' Misuzu's eyes reddened as she spoke.

'What?'

He remembered the sombre air in the classroom and the students' solemn faces.

'It can't be true,' he muttered, his comparison of the classroom atmosphere to a death now haunting him.

This isn't something to joke about.

Tears began to flow from Misuzu's eyes.

'After what happened yesterday, we went to a cafe in Jimbocho to cheer Kanna up. She was feeling low, but she was also happy that she managed to give you the chocolate.'

The accident had happened on her way home. Kanna was crossing the street on her bicycle when a minivan nearly hit her. The driver was watching a video on a phone mounted on the dashboard. A clear case of distraction.

The minivan was turning, and not going particularly fast, but fearing it wasn't going to stop, she braked, and at that moment another bicycle crashed into her from behind at full speed. The cyclist was looking at a map app and not paying attention. The impact threw her off balance. She was propelled sideways into the minivan. Fortunately, she wasn't caught under the wheels but she fell, striking her head hard.

Misuzu paused to wipe away tears with her palm.

'So, she's in the hospital now . . .'

'In the hospital?'

'Yes,' Misuzu replied. 'They said her life isn't in danger . . .'

Okishima felt the urge to blurt out, 'So, she's not dead, then?' but he caught himself just in time. It felt inappropriate.

'Which hospital?'

'Kanda General. But the doctor said she can't have visitors yet.'

'Right, thanks.'

Though the prospect of confessing his feelings had vanished for the moment, at least the worst hadn't come to pass. And, knowing that her injuries weren't life-threatening, a thought crossed his mind: if she's in hospital, there might be more chances to be alone with her.

'Anyway, I'll let you know when visitors are allowed, so please come and see her. I think she'd be happy to see you, even if you like Izumi,' Misuzu said.

'Ah, about that . . .'

Okishima explained the whole story.

'What? The feelings are mutual?'

'Ah, well, I guess that's one way to put it,' he replied, his ears turning red at the mention of mutual feelings. While he felt slightly guilty about Hayashida, who also had feelings for Kanna, the confirmation of mutual affection with Kanna brightened his spirits. Now, all that was left was to clear up the misunderstanding.

But days went by and still no permission for visitors was granted. The thorough medical examinations were taking longer than expected.

'Does it usually take this long?'

'I asked her mum over the phone, and it seems that she has disturbed brain waves and the cranial impact was in a vulnerable location, so they're just taking extra precautions. With spring break approaching and hardly any real classes left, it might be better for her to get the care she needs instead of rushing back to school,' Misuzu told him. Since she had found out about Okishima and Kanna's mutual feelings, they occasionally discussed how Okishima might confess to Kanna once he could visit her.

Then the new school term arrived.

Kanna's name was not on the list for the class changes. According to their previous form teacher, she had lost several years of memories due to the concussion. Although she was physically well, her family had decided to transfer her to a school in her father's home town to recuperate.

Early spring 2019

'Initially, I thought she'd regain her memories in a couple of months,' Okishima said quietly with a sigh as his eyes followed the movement of the second hand on the large pendulum wall clock in front of him.

Fumiko, who had been listening to his story, covered her mouth with both hands, tears welling up when she heard about Kanna's accident. She showed relief that Kanna was alive but was at a loss for words upon learning about the partial amnesia.

'So, what happened to her?' Fumiko asked, practically on the edge of her seat.

'She never came back,' Okishima replied quietly.

'Oh no.'

'Even now, the lost memories may still not have returned. But the accident only affected her recent memories – her family and childhood memories remained intact. I'm sure she managed to adapt after some initial confusion.'

'It's such a shame . . . especially since your feelings for each other were mutual,' Fumiko said sympathetically. But she regretted saying those words as soon as they left her lips. After all, it was Okishima who had suffered the most in all this. She also felt angry at herself for making him talk about the past out of mere curiosity.

How would I feel if Goro lost all memory of the time between meeting me and deciding to marry, totally forgetting that I ever existed?

'That's why I went back to the past. To meet Kanna before she lost her memories.'

Autumn 2012

Since Kanna left, a whole summer had passed. None of his classmates ever mentioned her – not even Hayashida, who was now cheerfully flirting with another girl. They had moved on, but Okishima couldn't let go.

There are moments in life that change everything, turning points that alter one's path. Yet it's rare to recognize them when they happen. More often than not, it's only in hindsight that a seemingly ordinary day reveals itself as pivotal.

Naturally, Okishima couldn't have known Kanna would be in an accident, let alone lose her memories. That day, his hesitation – and the embarrassment of being seen – had kept him from following her. It was a choice that would haunt him. If only he had known. If only he could have seen the future. But without such foresight, he was left to live with his regret.

One day in autumn, he visited the cafe where Kanna had stopped before her accident and lingered there for hours. He felt it was somewhat pathetic to cling to the past like this, but moving on was beyond him. The only other people in the cafe were a woman in a white dress seated at the furthest table and Kazu Tokita, the waitress, polishing cutlery behind the counter.

In most cases, a junior-high student sitting alone for hours would raise suspicion, prompting staff to check in. But Kazu didn't. For Okishima, this cafe was the one place where he could be alone with his thoughts, undisturbed.

He checked the time on his phone. Just past 7.30 p.m.

Is it really that late? I should head home.

He knew that the cafe closed at 8 p.m. As he was about to

get up from his seat, he noticed that he had barely touched his orange juice. The ice had melted completely, leaving a clear film of water on the surface. *Might as well finish it.*

Resigned, he sat back down and took a sip.

CLANG-DONG

'Hello, welcome,' Kazu called out at the sound of the bell.

It was the first customer to arrive since Okishima entered the cafe. The newcomer was a short man in his early thirties, wearing a suit and slightly out of breath – perhaps he had hurried, mindful of the cafe's impending closing time. He stood hesitantly at the entrance, still catching his breath, as if unsure whether to sit down. Kazu made no move to guide him to a seat.

Something feels off.

Okishima couldn't shake the strange vibe coming from the man. He watched him intently, forgetting his orange juice.

'Um.'

'Yes, how can I help?'

'Well, er . . .' The man started to speak, then hesitated, casting a quick, uneasy glance at Okishima. It was as if he had something to say – but didn't want Okishima to hear.

After a brief pause, he took a hesitant step towards the counter, then another. Lowering his voice, he finally asked, 'I heard that coming to this cafe can send you back to the past. Is that true?'

The cafe was small, it would be full with just nine people,

so even though the man spoke quietly, Okishima could hear him, but he could hardly believe what he'd said.

What? Go back to the past? Did I hear that right?

The man's question was so surreal that Okishima spun around, the jerky movement of his elbow almost knocking his glass over. His gaze flicked past the man to Kazu, who stood in the background, calmly polishing the cutlery as if nothing unusual had been said.

Okishima couldn't help but feel sorry for the waitress, thinking, *She must be troubled about how to handle this difficult customer.*

But to his surprise, Kazu just replied with a calm, matter-of-fact tone, 'You can return to the past, yes.'

Kazu's straightforward answer – so calm, as if such a thing was perfectly normal – made Okishima wonder whether he had misheard the question.

Did I really hear her say that he could return to the past? Wait – maybe there's a place called 'The Past' and this cafe sells some kind of special ticket for it? Intrigued and confused, he listened attentively to their conversation.

'Please, send me back! Three days ago – I was late to a client meeting, and the deal fell through! Our company is small, and the loss was huge. We're on the verge of bankruptcy! I'm begging you, send me back to that day, so I can make it to the negotiation on time! Please – I'm begging you!'

Hearing the man's desperate plea, Okishima understood why he had rushed in even though it was just before closing. Still, the idea of being able to return to the past seemed far-fetched. Talk about a drowning man clutching at straws – was this not the craziest attempt to escape the bitter reality of his company's impending collapse?

Even as a junior-high student, Okishima couldn't help but scoff. *If going back to the past was that easy, no one would have to struggle.*

But deep down, he was considering how he could redo what had happened on Valentine's Day. For just a moment, a thought flickered through his mind – *If I could go back to that day . . . maybe I could change it.* But as quickly as this fleeting hope came, he dismissed it – *No, that's impossible.*

He gulped his orange juice, trying to wash away Kazu's unsettling words.

'Thanks for the juice,' he said as he stood and made his way to the register, money in hand. The businessman glared at him, annoyed at the interruption.

Kazu, sensing his urgency, replied calmly yet ambiguously. 'It is indeed possible to go back to the past. You can return, but . . .'

As she spoke, she took the money from Okishima.

'But?' the man pressed, his eyebrows knitting together in confusion.

'You can go back to the past, but you cannot leave this cafe once you are there.'

'What?' The man's face fell, clouded with dismay.

'Also, no matter what efforts you make in the past, it's impossible to change the present,' Kazu continued, her hands busy with the cash register.

'What do you mean I can't change the present? What's the point then?' The man's expression grew more severe, but Kazu didn't look up from her task as she continued calmly.

'Even if you could go back and then leave the cafe and attend that crucial meeting on time, it wouldn't change the reality that your company is on the brink of insolvency.'

'That means there's no point in going back!' the man exclaimed in a burst of anger.

Despite his fury, Kazu remained composed and simply replied, 'That's true.'

The man's shoulders shook with rage as he shouted, 'What kind of place is this? It's a scam!' With that, he stamped out of the cafe, his footsteps echoing behind him.

CLANG-DONG

The door swung shut. Okishima stood frozen, still processing the confrontation, until Kazu's voice brought him back to reality.

'You're still planning to leave?' she asked.

This struck Okishima as an odd thing to say, considering he was already at the cash register. Normally, she would say something like, 'That'll be three hundred and twenty yen for the orange juice,' and hand him his change. Instead, it was as if she expected him to do something before leaving.

A sudden thought nagged at him – *Check it out.*

Compelled by this thought, he turned his gaze towards the seat where he guessed Kanna had sat on Valentine's Day.

'Can you really go back to the past?'

'Yes,' Kazu replied without hesitation. 'However, besides what I told the last customer, there are several other rules you should know,' she continued, handing back Okishima's money and cancelling the numbers she'd entered into the register.

Kazu then told him the other rules for time travel in the cafe.

1. The only people you can meet in the past are those who have visited the cafe.
2. Nothing you do while there will change the present.
3. The chair that takes you there is occupied by another customer, so you must wait until it is vacated.
4. Once in the past, you may not rise from the chair.
5. Your visit to the past, which begins with the pouring of the coffee, must end before the coffee gets cold.

After hearing Kazu's five additional rules, Okishima thought, *With all these rules, would anyone still want to go back to the past?* He could understand why the businessman had stormed out.

Despite his scepticism about the whole notion, the thought that Kanna had been to this cafe was enough to spur him on.

Even if I can't change the present, meeting Kanna before she lost her memories might be enough. Maybe I can clear up the misunderstanding from Valentine's Day . . . and finally tell her I like her. Even if this whole time-travel thing is just a lie, I've got nothing to lose. I want to go back to that day.

Okishima felt resolute but he still had many questions.

'To go back to the past, I have to sit in a specific seat, right? Which one is it?'

'That one.' Kazu pointed to the table at the far end of the cafe. A woman in a white dress sat there, quietly reading a book – just as she had been since Okishima arrived.

'So, I just need her to give up the seat, right?'

'Exactly.'

Okishima looked at the woman. It was the kind of weather outside where a coat was necessary, yet her white dress was short-sleeved.

Now that I think about it, that woman always wears the same dress.

Noticing his puzzled expression, Kazu said casually, 'She is a ghost.'

'A ghost?' Okishima's eyes widened. He didn't have time to question it, though – it wasn't his biggest concern right now.

Shaking off his surprise, he replied matter-of-factly, 'Oh, OK,' before moving on to the more pressing question on his mind.

'Exactly how long do I have before the coffee cools down? Is it around fifteen minutes, or less?'

He had been mentally rehearsing how he could clear up the misunderstandings with Kanna, just in case her memory came back. He estimated that it would take about fifteen minutes to explain everything thoroughly – including the fact that Hayashida also had feelings for her. If she was receptive, that would be enough, but if not, he'd need another fifteen minutes to convince her he had no romantic feelings for Izumi. All together, he thought he'd need about thirty minutes.

The reply Kazu gave him, however, was disheartening.

'The perception of time is so subjective, I can't give you an exact number. Some people who've gone back say they had about ten minutes, while others claim they didn't even get three.'

'I see,' Okishima muttered, his shoulders slumping a little as he glanced once more at the seat where the woman in the white dress sat.

If that's how it is, I should at least tell her how I feel.

He made up his mind.

'I understand the rules now. Please, I'd like to go back to the past,' he said, bowing his head politely.

'OK then.' Kazu nodded.

Then, as if on cue . . .

Flap. The sharp sound of a book closing echoed through the quiet cafe.

Okishima watched as the woman stood up. She had feet like a normal person, which didn't match his image of a ghost. She slipped through the narrow gap between the table and chair and started walking, but what struck him as odd was that her footsteps made no sound. As he watched her all he could hear was the rhythmic ticking of the large pendulum wall clocks and the faint rustle of his uniform.

The ghosts he imagined were like those in traditional Japanese paintings – ethereal, with translucent bodies you could pass your hand through as if touching air. But this woman's form looked as solid and ordinary as any human's. If he reached out, he was sure he could touch her. Fighting the urge to tap her shoulder and call out, Okishima just watched as she took the exit towards the toilet.

He couldn't shake the uneasy feeling that maybe it was all just a trick. No matter what Kazu said, the woman didn't seem like a ghost at all.

But when Kazu gently urged him to take the seat, he slid into the chair. After ensuring he was seated, Kazu quietly slipped into the kitchen, leaving the cafe empty except for him.

CLANG-DONG

He could hear Kazu's faint 'Hello, welcome' from the kitchen. It was so faint, he wondered if her greeting reached the entrance. The idea of a new customer left him awash with unease. What if they asked why he was sitting there? His gaze darted towards the kitchen, hoping Kazu would come back soon, and he almost called out to her. But, as is so often the case, his worries were unfounded. The tall man who stooped to enter the cafe was not a customer.

'Oh, hello, welcome,' the man said in a deep voice, nodding at Okishima. It was Nagare Tokita. He was in a stark white cook's uniform topped with a dark-toned Japanese-design bomber jacket and was carrying a shopping bag.

'Sorry I'm late,' he called out as he headed for the kitchen, not mentioning that Okishima was sitting in the seat that supposedly allowed time travel.

Okishima had never seen such a tall man before and he watched until Nagare disappeared. Then Kazu returned, carrying a tray with a shiny silver kettle and a white cup.

Nagare peeked out from behind her and asked, 'High-school student?'

'Junior high.'

'What class?'

'Third year.'

'Got it. You OK with coffee?'

'I think I can manage.'

'If it's too bitter, you can add sugar or milk. It won't affect the temperature, so don't worry . . . Oh, and the sense of time feels different for each person, so you should touch your cup around seven minutes in. Also, while you're back in the past, it's good to check the time on that clock at the far end.'

He pointed towards the pendulum wall clock at the back of the cafe that appeared to have its second hand motionless. Okishima, noticing this, began, 'Ah, but . . .'

'Right now, yes, but when you go back, that clock will be working,' Nagare added quickly.

Despite the strangeness of the situation, Okishima found the information about the coffee's cooling time of approximately seven minutes to be the most crucial detail.

'Thank you.'

'Yeah, you're welcome,' Nagare replied with a satisfied nod and narrowed his thin eyes.

'Are you ready?' Kazu asked, standing next to Okishima's table.

'Yes.' Okishima's gaze was fixed on the pristine white coffee cup before him. In the cafe's dim light, it seemed to emit an eerie, pale glow.

'Right then.' Kazu reached for the silver kettle. 'Before the coffee gets cold,' she murmured.

Okishima felt the atmosphere tighten sharply in a single moment as the silver kettle moved gracefully above the cup and came to a stop. As Kazu tilted it slowly, a thin stream of dark-brown coffee flowed from the spout.

Can I really go back to the past? He was still half doubtful, yet the thought of meeting Kanna from that day again stirred up a mixture of excitement and anticipation.

The final drop fell from the spout and the cup was filled. Ripples spread across the surface of the coffee, and a wisp of steam gently rose towards the ceiling.

As Okishima watched he felt dizzy and his vision swayed. *The scenery is . . .*

It seemed to be flowing from ceiling to floor, as if he was watching a slow-moving film reel.

Early spring 2019

'When I woke up, Kanna was sitting right there,' Okishima said, pointing to the table closest to the entrance. Fumiko followed his finger curiously. 'Honestly, I never really believed I could travel back in time.'

'You didn't?' Fumiko's eyes widened in surprise.

'When I saw her, it felt unreal. You know how sometimes in dreams you suddenly realize it's just a dream?'

'Yes, I know exactly what you mean.'

'That's how it felt. I still vividly remember the sensation,' Okishima said softly, recalling that moment seven years earlier. 'The first thing I did was pinch my cheek, just to check if it was real.'

'Do people really do that?'

'I did,' Okishima admitted with a slight blush.

Since ancient times, pinching one's cheek has been a common method to test whether something is a dream or reality. However, many people report feeling pain, smelling scents, or sensing heat in their dreams, so strictly speaking, determining reality based on whether a pinch causes pain is not entirely reliable. Fumiko knew this, but she chose not to mention it – because she, too, had once returned to the past.

'And then?'

'It hurt. And when I touched the cup, it was surprisingly lukewarm.'

'I know what you mean.'

Fumiko had also noticed that the coffee served just before travelling back in time was cooler than expected.

'I panicked a bit and looked at the clock at the end of the room. It was 6.21 p.m., so I decided to check the temperature before it hit the thirty-minute mark.'

His younger self, seven years earlier, had followed Nagare's advice to keep track of time.

Fumiko thought his calm actions sounded impressive for a

junior-high student, but she always wanted to hear the conclusion first and the details later, so she asked eagerly:

'Well, did you manage to clear up the misunderstanding?'

'Actually,' Okishima hesitated, scratching his head, 'I didn't.'

'What?' Fumiko exclaimed, her voice louder than it had been all day. 'You met her, right?'

'Yes, I did meet her.'

'So then, what happened?'

'I had forgotten something.'

'Forgotten what?' Fumiko's interest intensified. She stood up from her counter seat and approached his table.

'That she was with someone else at that time . . .'

'Ah!' The realization struck her. 'Her friend who called you from the classroom?'

'Yes. Kanna was at the cafe with Misuzu Horie.' Okishima smiled wryly and muttered, 'Seven minutes was just too short.'

'That's so unfortunate . . .' Fumiko sighed deeply, then gazed upward with a contemplative look.

14 February 2012

'Okishima?'

The sound of his name jolted him back to awareness.

'Why are you here?' Misuzu's voice was tinged with both surprise and suspicion. She was sitting at the table closest to the entrance and across from her sat Kanna, her presence only now coming into focus for Okishima.

Misuzu fixed him with a bewildered and slightly accusatory stare. He had appeared suddenly at the furthest table in the cafe, and to anyone unfamiliar with the peculiarities of the cafe it would have looked as if he had performed a magic trick or teleported.

Okishima wasn't as surprised. The moment he saw Kanna, he thought it must be a dream, which made it easier for him to accept the surreal scenario. He recalled scenes from mystery novels where someone was knocked unconscious with chloroform. Maybe the steam rising from the cup had a similar effect, putting him to sleep in an instant.

He looked around the cafe. The only people there were himself, Misuzu, Kanna, and Nagare behind the counter.

Misuzu stood up and walked towards Okishima. 'Hey, answer me. Why are you here?' As she closed the distance between them, a faint, pleasant scent – perhaps from her shampoo – drifted through the air, and he felt uneasy. He had always believed that pain and smell couldn't be experienced in dreams.

This is a dream . . . right? He pinched his cheek.

'It's not a dream.' Before the pain even registered, Nagare's voice had rung out from behind the counter.

It definitely hurts . . . And . . . Okishima touched the white cup in front of him. *It's not hot. It's lukewarm. This coffee is lukewarm.*

'What day is it today?' he asked Nagare.

'Today is the 14th of February 2012,' Nagare replied,

and pointed to the large pendulum wall clock near the entrance.

6.22 p.m.? No, 6.23 p.m. . . .? I remember him saying something about the coffee cooling down in about seven minutes. This is bad. Okishima felt a surge of panic.

'Er, well . . . how am I supposed to explain this? Um, actually—'

Misuzu cut him off. 'I never would have called you out of the classroom if I knew you liked Izumi.'

Her interruption caught him off guard, and he faltered. Behind her, Kanna sat with her head down, refusing to meet his eyes.

'No, that's not it. What I mean is, what Hayashida said back then was . . .'

He struggled to find the right words to clear up Kanna's misunderstanding. But this was reality, not a dream, and Misuzu's accusatory attitude only made him more muddled.

'What? If you've got something to say, just say it.'

'Er, well . . .'

As he tried to process what was happening, Misuzu hit him with eight shocking words: 'Kanna's liked you this whole time, you know?'

'What?'

His heart pounded like a drum, and his face grew hot.

Kanna shot to her feet and said, 'I've just remembered I have something to do.' Tossing some coins onto the table, she hurried out without another word.

CLANG-DONG

'Kanna?'

Misuzu realized that her words had embarrassed Kanna enough to make her leave. She rushed back to the table and picked up the coins Kanna had left behind. 'How much is it?' she asked Nagare.

'Nine hundred and eighty yen for the lemon squash and the tea.'

'All right, here.'

Misuzu slipped the coins into her purse and placed a one-thousand-yen note on the change tray. Nagare worked the register with a clatter and handed her the change while casting occasional glances at Okishima.

She just left, but . . . is he OK?

Misuzu took the change, deliberately ignoring Okishima, and walked out of the cafe.

CLANG-DONG

It happened in an instant.

The hands of the pendulum wall clock near the entrance pointed to 6.27 p.m. There was still a little time left before the coffee turned completely cold. The cafe, now empty except for them, had fallen into a deep silence. Okishima stood frozen, staring at the entrance.

'Wait here for a second.' Nagare stepped out from behind the counter, ready to chase after Kanna.

'Oh, it's fine,' Okishima murmured weakly.

'But you came all this way to see her . . .' Nagare hesitated, glancing from the entrance to Okishima and back. *Should I chase after her, even if it means forcing it? But . . . the time—*

He checked the clock again. 6.28 p.m.

If I go now, I might just make it.

As the owner of the cafe, Nagare had seen visitors from the future before. Each of them had arrived carrying their own thoughts, their own reasons.

The boy looked to be around thirteen or fourteen. For someone so young to have come here with his own resolve, only to be sent back to his present without fulfilling his purpose – it was too cruel.

Steeling himself, Nagare turned to Okishima and told him, 'I'll bring the girls back right now.'

Just then—

'Ah.'

Before Nagare could stop him, Okishima drained his coffee in one gulp.

Nagare watched as he tipped his head back, staring at the ceiling, and was overcome with an unbearable sense of frustration.

'Why did you do that?'

'It's fine. My time was up anyway, and besides . . .'

Okishima had believed that if he conveyed his feelings, something would change.

But in reality, after this, Kanna would be involved in an accident and lose her memories. Even if the misunderstanding between them was cleared up, it wouldn't change what was destined to happen. Even if he managed to tell Kanna that he loved her, she would forget it all.

Why did I only now realize something so important?

The emptiness, the sadness – it was too much for him. Instead, he muttered weakly, 'I was a fool for hoping.'

Nagare felt a sharp pain in his chest. As the owner of this cafe, he was consumed by his own helplessness. Maybe he could have called out to the girls before they left. Even if he couldn't stop them, if he had chased after them immediately, Okishima might not have drunk the coffee.

As a member of the Tokita family, Nagare had witnessed many people's stories unfold in this cafe. Even if he couldn't change the present, he had always hoped – at the very least – that their experiences here would have some kind of meaning.

But this time, there was nothing he could do. *Poor guy, it turned into an event that was just painful for him.* Nagare could only watch as Okishima's body turned into steam.

CLANG-DONG

As Okishima's consciousness began to fade, the doorbell rang, followed by the rapid patter of small footsteps rushing into the cafe.

It was Kanna, out of breath.

'Okishima!'

'Ozaki . . .'

By this point, half of Okishima's body had already begun dissolving into mist. But he was still conscious.

Kanna ran straight to the table where he sat and, with a voice that echoed through the entire cafe, declared—

'Okishima, I like you! Please go out with me!'

Her gaze was unwavering, filled with certainty, as she looked straight at him.

'Ozaki!' Okishima also shouted.

But Okishima's consciousness was fading. Time was running out.

'I also . . .' He tried to say, *'I like you,'* but stopped himself.

If I express my feelings now, and she forgets them anyway . . .

He struggled to keep his rising body anchored in place but the scenery around him flowed from ceiling to floor, and Kanna's figure became less and less visible.

Hold on! Until the day Kanna remembers this very day!

In his fading consciousness, Okishima shouted with all his might.

'I'll be waiting here on White Day! No matter how many years pass, I'll be waiting here on White Day! When you remember, come to meet me . . .'

But before he could finish, his body, turned to steam, was sucked up towards the ceiling.

'What? Okishima?' As the steam disappeared, the woman in the white dress reappeared where he had been.

Kanna could not comprehend what had just happened. She turned to Nagare.

'Where's Okishima? Where did he go?'

'Perhaps, if you come here on White Day, you might understand,' he answered gently, and narrowed his eyes into a smile.

Early spring 2019

'Wait, what? So, you mean you've been waiting all this time? Waiting for her to regain her memories and come here?'

'Yes,' Okishima admitted, somewhat embarrassed.

There was no guarantee that Kanna's memories would return to her. Even if they did, it was not certain she would come to this cafe because, over these seven years of memory loss, life continued. It wouldn't be strange if she fell in love with someone else.

Knowing all this, Okishima still visited this cafe every White Day, on the 14th of March.

Fumiko finally understood why Nagare had said, 'Is it that time of year already?' to Okishima when he appeared in the cafe, and the way he faced the entrance, watching it while turned away from the seat where he'd travelled back in time.

Seven years . . .

Fumiko's eyes shimmered with tears. She had returned to the past to meet Goro, who had left for America in pursuit of his dreams after saying goodbye to her.

'*Wait for me for three years*,' he told her. When he came back, they would get married. Goro's dream was to develop a type of game called an MMRPG. But three years later, when he returned from America, his talent had been recognized, and this time, he left for Germany. No one knew when he would return.

Fumiko wanted to support his dream, but she felt the loneliness of living apart.

I'm being selfish.

Even though they were separated, their feelings for each other were strong, and she had no doubt about their future together. She was not like Okishima, who continued waiting for Kanna not knowing whether he would ever see her again.

She stared at the entrance, wishing with all her heart for the doorbell to ring and for Okishima's beloved to appear.

'You sure you don't need to get back to work?'

Nagare had returned from the back room after putting Miki to sleep.

'Oh!'

Fumiko was a regular, so she knew to check the time on the centre clock. It was 2.45 p.m. – about thirty minutes after she had planned to return to the office.

'I need to go back! But . . .'

An overwhelming urge to see whether Okishima's long-awaited person would show up made her stamp her foot like a child throwing a tantrum.

'It's three hundred and eighty yen for the coffee,' Kazu said mercilessly from behind the register, urging her to pay.

'Ugh . . .'

'Time, time.'

'I know.'

At Nagare's prompting, Fumiko finally forced herself to get up and settle the bill.

Okishima watched her with a wry smile.

As she reached the entrance, she turned back and smiled reassuringly.

'She'll come. I'm sure of it.'

'I hope so,' Okishima replied, but the moment the words left his mouth, he caught himself.

He had told his friends about this before but none of them believed that he had travelled to the past; and most of them had dismissed the idea that Kanna would ever show up to see him even if she did regain her memories. No one had ever said with certainty, *She'll come*, the way Fumiko just had.

And in that instant, he realized – after these seven long years, a part of him had started to believe she might never come at all.

When he looked up, Fumiko reassured him once more with conviction: 'It's OK. She will definitely come.'

She clenched her fist as a sign of determination.

'Thank you,' Okishima said, standing up and bowing deeply.

Closing time

Okishima had just finished his second novel of the day. He was the only customer left in the cafe, aside from the woman in the white dress seated behind him. Kazu had just stepped out to take down the sign.

Dong-dong-dong-dong . . .

The large clock in the centre of the cafe began striking eight. With a quiet sigh, Okishima stood up to put the two books into his bag.

. . . dong-dong-dong-dong.

Okishima slowly took in his surroundings – the warm glow of the lampshades, the soft yellowish hue of the earthen walls, the deep, polished black of the wooden beams and pillars, and the ceiling fan turning above. Nothing had changed since he first stepped into this cafe seven years ago. It felt as if time had stopped here, and for a brief moment, he had the strange sensation that his junior high school self overlapped with the present.

CLANG-DONG

The doorbell rang. He assumed it was Kazu returning from putting away the sign.

Picking up his bill, Okishima turned towards the entrance and called out, 'Thank you for everything.'

However, it wasn't Kazu. It was a tall, reserved-looking woman. The bill fluttered from Okishima's hand.

They stood motionless, eyes locked.

'Did you wait?' she asked.

'No,' Okishima replied, reaching into his bag to pull out a box tied with a ribbon.

'Happy White Day . . .'

He held out the box to her.

The woman smiled quietly and accepted it.

'How nice,' she said.

Tock . . .

The minute hand of the pendulum wall clock made a sound as it moved forward, and time seemed to start moving again for the two of them.

III

The Secret

'Hey, don't you think Kazu's been acting a bit strange lately?' Fumiko Kiyokawa whispered to Nagare Tokita. She had waited to get him alone as what she had to say wasn't for Kazu's ears.

'What?'

Just moments earlier, Fumiko had been lamenting how a few of the new recruits at her company had come down with the 'May blues' and resigned – and how the whole thing was giving her a stomach-ache. This shift into a completely different topic caught Nagare by surprise.

'You haven't noticed?'

'Er . . . no, not at all,' Nagare admitted honestly.

'Kazu's been spacing out a lot lately, don't you think?'

'What do you mean?'

'It's like . . . her mind's somewhere else, like she's not really here. I'm not sure how to put it, but she's definitely acting strange.'

'Really? She's always been a bit like that, though . . .'

Nagare and Kazu were cousins. They had been brought up together. Kazu often called him her 'big brother', and ever since her mother transformed into something from which she would never return, Nagare had looked after her as if she was his sister.

Kazu spacing out hadn't started recently, but Nagare couldn't grasp what Fumiko was getting at and looked confused.

'Could it be . . .' Fumiko lowered her voice unnecessarily. 'Could it be she's waiting for Koku to show up?'

Fumiko and Nagare were well aware that Koku had feelings for Kazu. Seven years ago he had visited the cafe after becoming interested in one of her paintings at his university's cultural festival. After about six months of regular visits, he asked Kazu to go out with him, but his feelings were not reciprocated. Nagare had witnessed the scene and remembered it well.

On the day in question, despite Nagare being right there in front of him, Koku entered the cafe, walked straight up to Kazu, and without the slightest hesitation, said: 'I'm really interested in you. Will you go out with me?'

It took Nagare by surprise. *When did these two get so close?*

But Kazu, unfazed by the abrupt proposal, replied without so much as a change in her expression. 'I don't have any feelings for you. And whatever may happen in the future . . . I just don't feel I have the right to accept anyone's love. I'm sorry – but I can't.'

The words 'whatever may happen in the future' caught Nagare's attention. He looked at Kazu and realized: *She's still thinking about Auntie Kaname . . .*

Kaname was Kazu's mother and was now the woman in the white dress – the ghost – who was seated in the chair that allowed time travel. When Kazu was seven, Kaname went back to the past to meet her late husband but never returned. It was Kazu who poured the coffee that day, and ever since then she had blamed herself for turning her mother into a ghost. So when she turned Koku down, her '*I don't feel I have the right*' sounded to Nagare less like an excuse and more like a resigned belief: she didn't deserve to be happy.

For that same person to now be waiting for Koku to come, as Fumiko suggested – *That's impossible.*

Fumiko didn't know that Koku had declared his feelings to Kazu, nor that he'd been turned down. To her, Kazu had always appeared as a waitress of few words, someone who had difficulty engaging with people. And yet she had the impression that Kazu seemed to be waiting for Koku to show up, although she wasn't entirely sure. It could just be her imagination – or maybe just a little wishful thinking, hoping it might be true because it would make a good story.

The look on Nagare's face made her withdraw her comment, as if she'd said something completely off the wall.

'Yeah, I suppose with Kazu, that's pretty unlikely . . . Just forget I said anything.' She reached for her half-finished coffee.

CLANG-DONG

Just as the discussion had run its course the entrance bell rang.

Normally, Nagare responded immediately to a new customer but this time it was the customer who called out first.

'Um . . . the sign said you're open, so . . .'

Nagare snapped to attention. 'Oh – welcome!'

He gestured for the customer to take a seat at the central table.

'Here you are,' he said, setting down a glass of water and presenting the menu. 'What would you like? Even if it's not on the menu, I can make it as long as we have the ingredients. Just let me know if there's anything you're in the mood for.'

The customer was captivated by the sheer size of the man looming above them rather than the offer to make something off-menu. Nagare was nearly two metres tall and the glass of water in his hand looked like a tiny sake cup.

Watching the customer gaze up at him, Fumiko smiled, a touch of nostalgia in her expression.

I probably had that same look on my face the first time I saw Nagare, she thought.

The petite woman introduced herself as Rikako Kabe. She was thirty-two, the same age as Fumiko, but her round, youthful face with a natural fullness under her eyes made her look four or five years younger. In contrast to Fumiko's sharp, striking beauty, Rikako had a softness about her – an almost girlish charm.

She had not wandered into the cafe by chance.

'I heard that if you come here, you can travel to the future . . . is that true?'

'The future, you say?'

'Y-yes . . .' Rikako nodded, a bit flustered at being addressed by Fumiko, who sat at the counter but didn't seem to be a member of staff.

'This is your first time here, right?'

'Yes.'

'And do you know the rules? Especially the things you need to be careful about if you're going to the future?'

Aware they were about the same age, Fumiko spoke with a casual tone. She wasn't the shy type to begin with, but after four years of frequenting the cafe, she had started to carry herself almost like one of the staff.

'Yes, I know the rules well . . . someone has explained them to me,' Rikako replied, glancing towards Nagare as if silently asking, *Is it all right to be answering this woman's questions?*

There was a clear defensive tone in her response to Fumiko, a total stranger.

But Fumiko didn't pick up on Rikako's unease in the slightest.

'Oh? Who is this someone? Do I know them?' she pressed on with cheerful curiosity.

There was no ill intent in Fumiko's tone, but being peppered with questions by a stranger was far from pleasant. Even so, Nagare didn't notice Rikako's discomfort either and made no move to intervene.

Suppressing a sigh, Rikako gave in and answered.

'Actually . . . I heard about it from an acquaintance of mine, Yaeko Hirai. She used to run a small bar around here . . .'

'Hirai? What? Seriously?' The moment she heard the name, Fumiko jumped to her feet, overjoyed.

'You know her?'

'Know her? Of course! She was here the first time I came to this cafe. She even explained the rules.'

'So, you've been to . . . the future?'

'No, I went to the past.'

'I see . . .'

Finding out Fumiko not only knew Hirai but was also claiming to have travelled to the past, Rikako lowered her guard slightly.

In fact Hirai used to be a regular at the cafe. In the same year Fumiko returned to the past, Hirai travelled to see her younger sister, who had died in a car accident. Afterwards, she closed her bar and returned to her hometown of Sendai to take over Takakura, an inn that had been passed down in the family for generations. She was now working there as its proprietor.

'Where did you cross paths with Hirai?' asked Nagare, joining the conversation.

'Oh, I was wondering about that too!'

Fumiko, unable to contain her excitement, plopped herself

down in the seat across from Rikako without so much as asking.

'Hirai was my club senior back in high school. We happened to meet again last year, back in Sendai.'

'I've got to ask, which club?'

'The flower-arranging club.'

'Ikebana?'

'Yes.'

'No way! I just can't see Hirai as the flower-arranging type!'

When Fumiko first met her, Hirai was wearing something so flashy she seemed like the last person who'd ever wear traditional Japanese clothing.

Fumiko had always pictured ikebana as something done by graceful, demure women in traditional kimono, so the thought of Hirai being in the flower-arranging club came as a surprise.

But Rikako, who didn't know the version of Hirai who used to run a cosy bar, quickly came to her defence.

'I always looked up to Hirai. She wasn't just great at ikebana, she also played the koto and was trained in the tea ceremony. Every time there was a flower-arranging competition, she'd win. She was such a big deal in our community. People even called her a prodigy!'

Her eyes brimmed with respect and awe for Hirai, and for a moment, Fumiko felt as if she was being silently rebuked.

'Oh, really? I didn't know Hirai was such a big deal . . .'

Fumiko drew her shoulders in, caught off guard by the sheer force of Rikako's admiration. She wasn't familiar with flower arranging, the koto or the tea ceremony, so she couldn't quite appreciate what made Hirai so remarkable.

Nagare cut in to steer the conversation back on track.

'Just so you know – if you go to the future, there's no guarantee you'll meet the person you're hoping to.'

Though the rumour about this cafe centres on travelling back in time, it's also possible to go forward, although far fewer customers choose that. After all, since there's no way of knowing whether the person they want to meet will actually be at the cafe in the future, it's a leap few are willing to take. Even if they agree to meet years ahead – on a set day, at a precise time – there's still no telling what might change. They might get held up at work, caught in traffic, or stuck with no train services because of a typhoon. They might even forget the promise altogether.

Since you can only stay in the past or future until your coffee gets cold, even a small delay could mean missing your chance.

And you only get one chance – whether it's to the past or the future. If you go and you miss them, that's it. There's no second try. That's the gamble you take when choosing the future.

If Hirai had explained the cafe's rules in detail, Rikako would've heard all this already. Nagare just wanted to be sure.

'Yes, I understand.'

There wasn't a hint of hesitation in her eyes.

After finishing high school, Rikako moved from Sendai to Yamanashi Prefecture when her father was transferred for work. She stayed in Yamanashi after graduating from university and got a job at a travel agency. From when she was a child, she had loved trains and made sure to buy the monthly timetable book without fail. It wasn't just packed with train schedules – it also included maps of major stations and even domestic flight timetables.

One of her favourite pastimes was planning imaginary train journeys, hopping from one line to another using only the timetable, and her talent became something of a legend on a high-school field trip to Nagasaki: during free time, she plotted a route using her timetable that turned out to be faster than the way a friend had found with a smartphone app.

Working at a travel agency was the perfect fit for someone like Rikako. Her meticulous planning and knack for time management quickly earned her praise. At just twenty-eight, she was promoted to branch manager, and by thirty, she was overseeing three prefectures as the area manager.

Rikako had run into Hirai again about six months ago. Though she usually handled planning and operations as the area manager, she sometimes led small group tours to hear directly from customers. On one such trip to Sendai, the group stayed at an inn called Takakura – run by none other than Hirai.

'Oh, is that you Rikako? It's been ages!'

While greeting the guests, Hirai noticed Rikako right away and called out cheerfully. It had been well over ten years since

Rikako had last seen her face, so it took a moment to recognize the inn's proprietor as Yaeko Hirai.

'It's me – Yaeko from the flower-arranging club!'

'Oh . . .'

A vivid image of Yaeko Hirai from high school sprang to mind.

She left home on bad terms and went to Tokyo, if I remember rightly . . .

Rikako had had no idea Yaeko was now running an inn, and her surprise was plain to see. But she was here with work – there were guests waiting.

Rikako dipped her head in formal politeness.

'Good afternoon. These are the guests from NGS.'

Yaeko immediately grasped her intent and bowed in turn.

'Welcome to Takakura. My name is Hirai. I am the proprietor.'

A wave of relief washed over Rikako. As she guided the group to their rooms, Yaeko leaned in close, her voice low against Rikako's ear.

'Let's talk later,' she whispered, then gave her a quick, playful wink.

It was such a dazzling, confident gesture that even Rikako – despite herself – felt her heart skip a beat. If not for that wink, she would have gone about her job as usual. But that one little wink had her heart fluttering like a schoolgirl's.

I don't want to let this moment slip away, she thought.

A tour guide's job doesn't leave much time for breaks – and Yaeko had her hands full as the proprietor.

In the end, they never found that moment to talk. Morning came, and it was time to check out.

Deep down, Rikako had resigned herself to the idea that it was just one of those polite things people say. Sure, they'd been in the same flower-arranging club – but that was seventeen years ago. They'd both grown up, moved on, built new lives. A chance reunion didn't make them old friends.

She'll probably forget all about me in a few days, she thought. Still, Yaeko's 'Let's talk later' lingered in her mind.

'Has anyone left anything behind?' she asked the group as she approached the lobby for checkout.

Even so . . .

Deep down, she did want to speak to Yaeko. Only – she hadn't gone looking for her. And before she knew it, it was time to board the bus. After a headcount, she gave the driver the signal. 'We're good to go.'

A knot tightened in her chest. *If Yaeko hadn't said, 'Let's talk later,' maybe this wouldn't feel so lonely.*

Just then—

'Rikako!'

She heard her name being called.

'Excuse me – please stop the bus!'

She bowed quickly to the startled passengers and stepped off. That's when she saw her: Yaeko, running towards her in a kimono.

'Yaeko!'

'I'm so sorry,' Yaeko said, breathless as she took Rikako's hand. 'I really wanted to talk, but I just couldn't find the time.'

Rikako felt a flush of shame. She had blamed Yaeko for her own loneliness. But more than that – she was grateful that Yaeko *had* found the time.

'Here – read this.' Yaeko pressed a letter into her hands. 'Come on, get back on the bus. You can't leave your guests waiting.' She turned to the driver and the group. 'Thank you – and I'm sorry, everyone!' Then, keen to spare Rikako any blame for the delay, she helped her up the steps onto the bus.

'Get in touch, OK? I'll be waiting.'

She waved as the bus began to move. The entire exchange had taken less than a minute.

That night, Rikako opened the letter. It began with the day she'd joined the flower-arranging club – how, standing among a group of first-years, she'd nervously introduced herself with a redundant, 'I'm Rikako Kabe, a first-year student,' and made everyone laugh. It recalled the questions she used to ask, and how she'd once mentioned buying the train timetable book every month.

The letter filled eight pages. Near the end, Yaeko wrote:

'I always had a feeling you'd end up working in travel. I was so happy to see you again after all these years – and to see you thriving as a tour escort. If you ever need anything, don't hesitate to reach out. Yaeko.'

She'd even written her phone number at the bottom.

A letter always carries the feelings of the one who writes it. Yaeko, while going about her duties running the inn, had used her scarce spare time to write this. While Rikako had simply waited in silence, Yaeko had kept her 'Let's talk later' promise – with a letter. Rikako wiped away a quiet tear. *She really is someone worth looking up to,* she thought.

'Wow, classic Hirai!' Nagare exclaimed, his arms crossed with admiration after hearing Rikako's story.

When she was a regular at the cafe, Hirai's small bar bustled with customers every night without fail. He remembered her once telling him that even if someone was a first-time visitor, she would remember their face and everything they talked about.

At the time, he had thought she was exaggerating. But she wasn't. Hirai remembered her time with Rikako with perfect clarity – despite it being a memory from seventeen years ago.

Only one question remained. Nagare had been so caught up in the tale of their reunion that he hadn't thought to ask.

But Fumiko was not about to leave it unasked.

'So, when exactly did you hear about this cafe from Hirai?'

'Oh right! Was it in her letter?' Nagare asked, following up.

'No, actually, Hirai told me only recently. I needed to consult her about something personal, so I took time off work and went to see her in Sendai. That's when she happened to mention it, and I got curious.'

'Did she tell you about the risk of going to the future? That you might not be able to meet the person you wished to see?'

'Yes, she did.'

'And you still want to go?'

'Yes.'

'Why? Oh, you don't have to say if it's too personal.'

Fumiko's line of questioning had steered the conversation back to the heart of the matter. The curiosity in her eyes made it clear that beneath her polite restraint she was yearning to know why.

'Honestly, I just kind of want to see the future . . .'

'That's all?'

'Yes. But, since I'm going anyway, I thought maybe I could bring back a train schedule as proof.'

'A train schedule?'

'Yeah, this.'

Rikako reached into her bag and pulled out a book about two centimetres thick.

'What's that?' Fumiko asked.

'A train timetable.'

'Oh, sorry. I can see that. But it says it's a monthly issue?'

'Yes. It's published every month.'

'Every month? Do train schedules really change that often?'

'Of course. I buy a new one every month.'

Rikako stated this as if it was the most obvious thing in the world.

Fumiko, not wanting to reveal how little she cared, simply replied, 'Wow, that's something.'

'But how are you going to get the timetable once you're in the future?' Nagare posed the question plainly. 'You can't leave the cafe, you know.'

But Rikako already had an answer ready. Without the

slightest hesitation, she smiled and said, 'That's easy. I'll just ask the cafe owner.'

'Hirai told you that?' asked Nagare.

'Yes.'

'I see . . .'

Nagare gave a small sigh, half-impressed and half-exasperated by Hirai's meddling.

Fumiko clapped her hands and burst into laughter.

'So, would that be all right?'

'Yeah, I guess . . . where can I get one of those timetables?'

There was no way he could say no now. Nagare gave in to Rikako's request. But not in a reluctant way – his expression was one of relief – her reason for going to the future was one of simple curiosity.

Most people who came to this cafe carried regrets so heavy they were impossible to undo. And yet, no matter how desperately someone tried to change the past, the present stayed the same.

And sending people off knowing that things couldn't be changed had taken a toll on Nagare. There were also those who gave up on returning to the past once they heard all the troublesome rules.

That's why someone like Rikako was rare. Unlike when Nagare's wife Kei had gone to see her daughter Miki, Rikako didn't have someone she longed to meet; she simply wanted a train timetable from the future. If that was all, then all Nagare had to do was remember the request. It was hardly a burden.

Compared to the emotional weight of sending off Hirai or Kei, this was easy on the heart.

'You can buy the timetable at any large bookshop,' added Rikako.

'Got it.'

Nagare nodded and reached under the register to retrieve a memo pad and pen so he could write down the date and time Rikako wanted to travel to.

'Now, sorry – could you tell me again when exactly you'd like to go?'

'Nagare, aren't you jumping the gun a little? She hasn't even . . .'

Fumiko trailed off, looking over at the woman in the white dress. Nagare followed her gaze.

'Ah, right.'

He scratched his head, embarrassed that he'd forgotten the rule: to go to the past or the future, one must wait for the woman in the white dress to leave her seat and go to the toilet.

'There's no way to predict when she'll get up, right?' Rikako asked – Hirai had clearly told her that too.

'That's right. It's difficult to say how long you need to wait, but I don't think she's gone yet today.'

Nagare glanced at the central pendulum wall clock. It was just past six in the evening. The cafe had three pendulum wall clocks, but only the one in the centre kept accurate time. the other two ran fast or slow.

'What time does the cafe close?'

'Eight o'clock. But if you're willing to wait, you're welcome to stay as late as you need.'

'That's a relief.'

'Are you staying overnight? At a hotel or something?' Nagare was concerned – Rikako had come from Yamanashi, more than a hundred kilometres away.

The woman in the white dress *did* go to the toilet once a day. But for her, midnight was not the line between one day and the next. There were times when it took until 1 a.m., and on the rare occasion, she did not to go until daybreak. Then, after the passing of only a few hours, she might go again. Chances were, she went to the toilet three hundred and sixty-five times a year – though it might be once more, or once less. That was the level of precision they were working with. Nagare was worried that Rikako might be planning to make the trip in a single day.

'Oh, yes. I've already checked in at a business hotel near the station.'

'Well, that's OK then.'

'Yes,' Rikako replied with a smile.

However, Rikako's reason for going to the future was not to pick up a train timetable – that was a lie. She had another reason entirely.

It was about a month ago that Rikako heard about the cafe from Yaeko. In Sendai, the cherry blossoms begin to bloom in

April. It was the height of tourist season, but Rikako had pulled some strings at work to take time off and visit the ryokan Takakura – Yaeko's traditional inn – in Aoba Ward, Sendai City.

She waited at the back entrance of the inn. Eventually, Yaeko appeared, dressed in a vivid red floral shirt and pure white skinny jeans. She looked like an entirely different person from when she wore traditional Japanese clothing. Her long hair was curled at the ends, her make-up was subtle – except for her lips, which gleamed a striking crimson. She had a high-end designer shoulder bag slung over one shoulder and a fur-trimmed coat draped over her arm.

'Sorry to keep you waiting.'

'Thank you again for making time for me.'

Rikako was dressed in a white blouse, a pastel-coloured cardigan, and a long denim skirt. Standing side by side, the two looked less like friends or sisters and more like mother and daughter.

'Thanks for fitting this around my day off.'

'Not at all – I'm the one who invited myself.'

'Well, let's get something to eat first, shall we?'

'Yes, let's.'

Soon after, a taxi pulled up in front of them, and the door opened.

Just as Rikako was marvelling at the perfect timing, Yaeko climbed confidently into the taxi and called out to the driver:

'Hi, Takiiiii . . . Take us to Koryuan, please.'

She must have called the cab before leaving Takakura. It seemed she knew the driver well.

Rikako was quietly impressed by Yaeko's flawless sense of timing and organization. Watching her profile, she thought, *Yaeko will definitely know the best answer to my problem.*

Koryuan was a refined restaurant near Takakura, known for its traditional Japanese cuisine. It was a favourite of Yaeko's. The interior was serene, with private rooms and a view of a seasonal garden.

When they arrived, they were led to the furthest room at the back. Perhaps because it wasn't yet dinner time, the restaurant was nearly empty. The room they were shown to – plain walls and no windows – was a compact four-and-a-half tatami mat space.

The attendant bowed.

'Your meal will be served later,' she said politely before quietly slipping away.

As soon as she sat down across the low table, Yaeko got straight to the point.

'So? What's going on?'

It was only then that Rikako realized – Yaeko had reserved this room especially for today.

All Rikako had written in her message was: 'There's something I'd like to talk to you about. Would you be willing to meet and hear me out?'

Normally, that wouldn't be enough to convey the weight of a conversation. But Yaeko had made sure to arrange a private space for just the two of them. When it comes to important matters, people often find it hardest to begin. The more serious the topic, the more and more they tend to skirt around it with idle chatter. The setting also plays a role. Had Yaeko taken her to a lively, bustling restaurant – or conversely, to a place so quiet that every word could be overheard by staff or other patrons – starting the conversation would have been far more difficult.

That they could speak so freely now was entirely thanks to her thoughtfulness: choosing a relaxing, private room at a traditional restaurant and even informing the staff in advance to give them space.

And once she had asked, 'What's going on?' there was no turning back.

Even if what Rikako had to say turned out to be nothing serious, she knew Yaeko would just laugh it off with that light, carefree charm of hers.

Rikako found herself once again captivated by Yaeko's quiet strength, her natural warmth.

And so, she decided – there was no need to dress it up.

'The truth is . . . the man I've been seeing for the past two years proposed to me. But then I found out, during a health check, that I have cancer. They told me there's a sixty per cent chance I'll still be alive in five years.'

The night before, she'd lain awake, endlessly turning the question over in her mind – *Is this really something I should burden Yaeko with?* Who wouldn't be caught off guard by such a sudden confession of 'I have cancer'? But she couldn't bring herself to tell her parents, or her sister – much less the man who had just asked her to marry him.

I don't want to worry my parents. If I tell my sister, it'll get back to them for sure. And him . . . He just proposed. I can't bring myself to crush that happiness with something like this.

And in that moment, Yaeko's face had come to mind.

Rikako sensed a perfect equilibrium in their friendship – intimate enough for trust, yet detached enough to safeguard secrets.

Close friends or colleagues might be connected somehow, and word could slip out. It might be a nuisance to Yaeko . . . but still, I just need someone to listen.

And the moment she told Yaeko about the cancer, the tears came. Big, wrenching sobs.

Her feelings of anxiety and fear about death, bottled up from being unable to consult with anyone, now surged out.

Her doctor had encouraged her, saying, 'Medicine has come a long way. Even with a sixty per cent five-year survival rate, if you stay focused on treatment, you'll be fine.' Clinging to that hope like a lifeline, she had scoured the internet, desperately searching for stories of full recovery. And still, nothing could allay her anxiety.

'I just . . . I couldn't accept his proposal, not while feeling like this . . .'

As she said it, fresh tears spilled down her cheeks.

'I see. That must have been hard for you.'

Yaeko slowly stood and sat down beside Rikako.

'If there's anything I can do, just say the word. It's going to be OK. You're going to be OK.'

Saying this, Yaeko gently pulled Rikako's head to her chest.

As she cried into Yaeko's embrace, Rikako gradually

began to calm down, and her feelings began to take shape into words.

'I think . . . what really hurts isn't the thought of dying. It's the thought that I might have to give up marrying him because of my illness.'

'Are you planning to turn him down?'

Rikako's voice rose sharply. 'Could you say it, Yaeko? Could you tell someone, "I might die, but please marry me anyway"?'

'Er . . .'

Rikako immediately regretted it. She knew Yaeko hadn't meant any harm, and she hadn't meant to lash out. 'I – I'm sorry.'

'It's OK,' Yaeko said calmly, without the slightest trace of anger. 'You're right. I'm not sure I could say it either.'

But Rikako could tell. She knew those were gentle words, a kind lie, meant only to comfort her. After a little while, Yaeko called for the attendant and had their meal brought in.

'When you eat something delicious, it gives you strength. Come on, let's eat,' she said cheerfully. Fresh tears welled up and spilled down Rikako's cheeks.

It was during the meal that Yaeko told her about the cafe where you could travel in time.

At first, Rikako was sceptical. But the more she listened to Yaeko's story – how she herself had travelled back – the more she found herself thinking, *It sounds like a fairy tale . . . but I just can't believe Yaeko would lie about something like this. Even if it's all made up, I'd still love to visit that cafe in Jimbocho she used to go to.*

Rikako had always loved travelling. It was a hobby of hers to seek out cafes wherever she went – quiet little places where locals gathered. Sitting there, breathing in the same air, she felt as if she could melt into the rhythm of the town. It brought her peace. It made her feel at home.

A cafe two floors underground, with no windows. Dimly lit by shaded lamps. Three towering pendulum wall clocks reaching all the way to the ceiling. Charming staff and delicious coffee. And in that cafe, you can slip back into the past . . . What a beautiful idea.

For a little while, Rikako even forgot about her illness, letting her heart drift to a different thought: *If I could go back . . . what moment would I choose?*

'But you know, there are some pretty annoying rules you have to follow if you want to go back to the past,' Yaeko said.

'Rules? What kind of rules?' Rikako asked, leaning in a little.

By the time their meal was nearing its end, Yaeko had begun explaining the conditions for travelling back in time. Rikako didn't fully believe her – yet she didn't dislike these kinds of fantastical stories either, so she listened with quiet interest.

'First, even if you return to the past, you can only meet people who have visited the cafe at least once.' To make it clear there were multiple rules, Yaeko held up her hand and folded down her thumb.

'Second, no matter how hard you try while back in the past, you can't change the present.

'Third, in order to return to the past, you have to wait until the woman in the white dress gets up to go to the toilet – hers is the seat you need to sit in.'

As she spoke, she folded down her index finger, then her middle finger.

Listening intently, Rikako tilted her head slightly, thinking, *You have to wait for someone to go to the toilet? Who exactly is this woman?*

Yaeko went on, folding down her ring finger and little finger as she added, 'And even after you go back to the past, you're not allowed to get up from that seat. Plus, there's a time limit. A waitress will pour you a cup of coffee, and that's when your time in the past begins. But you can't stay long – only until the coffee gets cold,' Yaeko finished with a wry smile, pouring sake into her cup.

'It's that short?'

'Over in a flash.'

'Right . . .'

'That's why,' Yaeko added, downing her sake in one gulp, 'once people hear all the rules, almost no one still wants to go back.'

Just moments earlier, Rikako had been daydreaming – wondering what time she would visit if she could return to the past, and what she might see. But hearing those rules, most of that curiosity simply faded away.

After that, the two of them hopped from place to place – three izakayas for snacks, two bars – drinking together until past three in the morning. Every spot they visited was one of

Yaeko's regular haunts, and just like at Koryuan, they were shown to private rooms where they could talk freely, just the two of them. Yaeko, who had once run a cosy bar in Tokyo, proudly declared herself a heavy drinker and kept up a brisk pace from the start, but Rikako didn't fall behind.

In the end, it was Rikako who, thinking of Yaeko's schedule, gently brought the night to a close.

'Yaeko, you have work tomorrow, don't you? I'm so sorry for keeping you out so late . . . I'm OK now.'

After Yaeko saw her back to her hotel by taxi, Rikako bowed deeply and said, 'Our talk today meant a lot – I truly appreciate it. As for the proposal . . . there's something I'd like to try first. After that, I'll decide whether to accept it or not. Thank you so much for everything today.'

Hearing this, Yaeko gave a satisfied smile and, in a voice slurred with drink, replied: 'Make sure you really understand what your boy feels, OK? 'Cause it's not me who can fill your heart – it's him, got it?'

Unlike Rikako, who stood composed and steady, Yaeko was swaying precariously, barely able to stay on her feet as she clutched the taxi door for support, her whole body rocking unsteadily.

'Um . . . right, well . . . goodnight then,' Rikako said, bowing again, though she could hardly make out what Yaeko was trying to say.

Then she turned and went into the hotel.

Once Rikako had disappeared from view, Yaeko collapsed

into the back seat of the taxi, mumbling with the last of her strength, 'Takiiiii . . . home . . . please . . .'

And then, almost immediately, she began to breathe in soft, rhythmic snores.

Once she reached her room in the hotel, Rikako pulled her planner out of her bag and checked her schedule. Her days off were irregular, and the soonest one was the following Tuesday. She glanced at the clock – it was just before four in the morning. In two hours, she would have to check out and head back to Yamanashi, then go straight to work in the afternoon.

She sighed. *I should have taken one more day off.*

But it wasn't because she dreaded the idea of going to work after drinking all night with Yaeko.

At Koryuan, after hearing about all the tedious rules, she had lost most of her curiosity about the cafe.

And yet – *I now want to go to that cafe where you can return to the past. I want to know what happens to me* – that desire had taken root.

Talking with Yaeko had helped Rikako sort through her feelings.

First:

It's not that I'm hesitating because I might die soon. I'm afraid that once he knows I might die, he'll regret proposing to me.

And second:

I can't bring myself to say, 'I might die within five years, but please marry me anyway.'

In other words, Rikako realized that her true, unclouded feeling at that moment was:

If it weren't for my illness, I would have accepted his proposal.

No one could know what would happen in five years.

If she refused him now, because of her illness, and then lived on past that point, she would surely regret her decision.

And in the end, she understood the truth behind her heart's desire:

What I want most . . . is proof that I'll still be alive five years from now.

But such a thing – knowing the future – was impossible, unless she actually travelled there. She had already resigned herself to that. At least, until she heard what Yaeko said that night.

It was at the second bar they visited. It was already past two in the morning. Yaeko's speech had grown slurred, her words loose and hard to follow.

'In that cafay, it wash Kei who . . . went to the future, you know . . . After I cam back from the pasht, she reminded me – real sharp, like – "Didn't you promish your little shishter?" Sho I'm really, really grateful to Kei . . . Alsho, if it washn't for her, I'd be a ghosht now . . .'

'Um . . .' Rikako leaned in.

'What is it?' Yaeko asked, blinking slowly.

'Could you tell me a little more about that?'

'Ghost?'

'No, not that part – Yaeko, you just said "went to the future", didn't you?'

'Future?'

'Yes! That! Please – could you tell me more?'

And that was how Rikako learned the truth from Yaeko: the cafe didn't just let you go back to the past. It could take you to the future too.

If I really can go to the future . . . Rikako felt her heartbeat quicken. *If it is even possible . . .*

Back in her room, she had regained a bit of composure. After all, Yaeko had been drunk when she said it. Rikako didn't want to let herself get carried away only to end up heartbroken later. At the very least, she needed to confirm whether it was truly possible to travel to the future.

She looked at the clock – 5 a.m.

She decided to get a little sleep before checkout. She wasn't feeling tired, but she would need to work that afternoon. She shrugged off her coat and lay down on the bed, then pulled out her phone and searched, 'Jimbocho cafe where you can return to the past'. The only thing that came up was a social media post from someone claiming they had gone back to see a pet who had died. The comments on the post were mostly critical, but the story itself stirred something warm inside Rikako's chest.

If it's just a regular cafe, I should be able to call after noon and ask. I can confirm it any time. The real question is . . .

The idea that she might be able to go to the future was like a beam of light cutting through the darkness. But there was a problem.

Even if I really could go five years into the future . . . how would I even confirm if I'm alive or not?

She let out a deep sigh and stared at the ceiling.

It was just past seven in the evening. Rikako had been waiting for the woman in the white dress to visit the toilet since six o'clock. She had remained seated at the centre table, where she had finished her dinner.

CLANG-DONG

A few moments later, Kazu Tokita appeared, having returned from helping with Kinuyo Mita's art class.

She was carrying a large canvas bag. Spotting Rikako, she gave a small bow and bestowed her usual greeting of 'Hello. Welcome,' and went on through to the back residence.

Kazu's voice had been soft, but Rikako recognized it. She was unmistakably the same woman who had answered the phone last month, when Rikako called to verify the story she'd heard from Yaeko.

Dong, dong . . .

Nine p.m.

Even an hour past closing time, Kazu remained quietly behind the counter. Rikako couldn't see exactly what she was doing, but it was clear from her movements that she was working on something with her hands.

As a tour conductor, Rikako was used to managing bus and train departures at travel destinations: her job demanded constant vigilance with time. That's why she couldn't help but wonder, *Is she stuck here because I'm still hanging around? If that's the case . . .*

But just as she began to feel anxious about it—

'Please don't worry,' said Kazu, as if reading her mind.

Startled, Rikako looked up.

'I live here,' Kazu said, turning her gaze towards the door to the back residence beside the kitchen. 'With my big brother.'

Come to think of it, the owner went into that room after she returned, and he hasn't come out since.

Rikako had come across several places where the shop and residence were under the same roof, so she understood that Kazu meant, *You don't need to worry about the time.*

'I – I see,' she replied.

Kazu nodded.

And then silence returned. The woman in the white dress showed no sign of standing, remaining perfectly still save for the occasional turn of a page. According to Yaeko, the woman in the white dress reliably got up to use the toilet once a day. But the longer Rikako waited, the more uncertain she became.

First came the doubt: *Can you really travel to the future?*

It wasn't that she didn't trust Yaeko, but she couldn't rule out the possibility that Yaeko had been duped.

Why am I hesitating now, after coming all this way? She questioned her own heart, searching for the source of her doubt.

Maybe I'm just afraid to know what's waiting in my future. She could no longer predict how she might feel once she knew. Her ideal resolve was to face death with calm acceptance and live out the rest of her days with purpose. But until she knew what was truly ahead, she couldn't be sure she had the strength to follow through.

If I'm going to back out, this is my last chance . . .

As she continued waiting for the woman in the white dress to stand, Rikako's resolve wavered again and again. The human heart shifts from moment to moment – even the strongest conviction can crumble with startling ease.

Rikako glared at the woman in the white dress, who still showed no sign of rising, her stare heavy with frustration.

And then—

Flap.

The woman closed the book she was reading. Slowly, she rose from the chair.

Rikako was startled. It felt as if the woman had heard her inner voice.

Then, as the woman in the white dress moved towards her and glided by her side, instead of the expected sound of footsteps, there was only silence.

Rikako couldn't move a muscle. It wasn't fear that held her still, but the weight of the decision she had to make: to go to the future or not. She had thought that once the woman in the white dress stood up her hesitation would vanish. But instead it deepened.

I don't want to go.

She clapped her hands over her mouth and tried with all

her might to swallow the words already forming on her lips: *I've changed my mind.*

Just then, 'I heard you came to travel five years into the future for a timetable.'

Kazu's voice gently broke the silence.

She was clearing the table where the woman in the white dress had been sitting.

'Ah – yes, that's right. But . . .'

Rikako floundered. She thought Kazu might be telling her to go ahead and take the seat. She felt far more flustered than she'd ever imagined. But what Kazu said next was the complete opposite of what she expected.

'If it's not something you need right away . . . why not come back another day?'

'Eh? No, but – I've already waited this long . . . now the seat's free . . .' Rikako faltered, her heart wanting to flee even as her words betrayed her: 'I'll sit. I'll go.'

'As you wish.'

Kazu glanced briefly at her, then lowered her eyes and quietly disappeared into the kitchen.

In that instant, Rikako regretted what she'd said.

Maybe I should have taken her advice and come back another day . . .

But then again—

Maybe this is for the best.

After all, she was just going to pick up a train timetable. She couldn't think of a single good reason to postpone that.

No need to despair. The five-year survival rate is sixty per cent.

That means the odds are still in my favour. Medical science is advancing fast. Who's to say they won't discover a groundbreaking new treatment next year? Progress always moves forward – it doesn't go back!

'Right!' she said aloud and sprang to her feet. But her knees trembled, and she couldn't take a step.

To shake off her doubt, she slapped both cheeks hard with the palms of her hands.

That's right! Come on, pull yourself together. If you run away now, you'll regret it for the rest of your life. If this is the life I've been given, then at the very end, I want to be able to say: I gave it everything I had.

She nodded firmly, then strode to the table where the woman in the white dress had been sitting and sat down with a determined thump.

'Would you like me to explain the rules?' Kazu had returned from the kitchen, carrying a tray with a pure white cup and a silver kettle.

From this silver kettle, coffee would be poured – and with that, one could travel to the past or the future.

'That's fine, I think I know everything I need to know.'

She had already gone over the rules countless times with Yaeko, even reread the notes she'd taken.

'OK, then.'

Kazu reached for the silver kettle.

At that moment, Rikako felt the air around Kazu tighten. She even thought that perhaps the temperature in the room had dropped ever so slightly.

Rikako repeated the most important rule in her mind.

First – no matter what I learn, I must drink the coffee to the last drop and return. Think about everything else after I get back. I can't become a ghost and bring sorrow to the man who knows nothing, or to Yaeko who told me about this cafe.

Kazu was watching Rikako closely. When their eyes met, she gave her a small nod.

'Then . . .'

She reset the moment, her voice low and measured.

'Before the coffee gets cold.'

The silver kettle in Kazu's hand came to a precise halt. Slowly, it tilted. From the spout, a stream of dark brown coffee poured into the pure white cup. Kazu's posture, the grace of her motion – it was like watching a ballerina. Beautiful, and uncannily still.

Rikako's attention was drawn to the sudden appearance of a delicate wisp of steam rising from the filled cup. And in the very next moment, she realized her body was floating. Not just floating—

My body . . . it's turning into steam!

There wasn't time to cry out. The scene surrounding her began to drift upward. And her steam-like form rose too, drawn ever higher until she was swallowed by the ceiling.

'I'd like to marry you . . . if that's what you want.'

Gaku Hanada's proposal was a perfect reflection of who he

was. On the one hand, you could say he was always thinking of Rikako's feelings. On the other, you might say he wasn't the assertive type.

Rikako, by contrast, was the type who never backed down once she'd made up her mind. They were opposites. But they weren't a bad match.

Rikako and Gaku met at a party hosted by the travel agency where they worked. He was introduced to her by their boss, Yajima. Unlike Rikako, who mainly handled domestic travel, Gaku dealt primarily with overseas clients.

He'd spent his student years as a backpacker, travelling the world solo. He'd stuck to a tight budget and carried everything on his back. Later, he took part-time jobs and whenever he'd saved up enough money he'd set off on an unplanned trip abroad. When he ran out of funds, he returned to Japan. That was his way of life.

It was this experience that got him hired at his current company. But he was conscientious by nature and he didn't want to cause any trouble at work, so even though he longed to travel again, he never took extended leave to go backpacking. His work ethic was solid, and people expected he'd rise through the ranks quickly. But he always declined, saying firmly: 'I'm not cut out to be in charge of anyone.' He preferred quietly doing the tasks he was given. That was the kind of man he was.

Yajima often invited the two of them out for meals or drinks. He had all but forced them to exchange contact information, but before long, Rikako was the one reaching out. She had never been abroad and Gaku's backpacking tales were endlessly fascinating.

Gaku's proposal was spurred on by one such dinner with Yajima. It was the first time in a long while for them to be dining with him, and he had suddenly asked, 'So? Are you two thinking about marriage?'

It was then he said it: 'I'd like to marry you . . . If that's what you want.'

If that's what you want – typical of Gaku, it was a wishy-washy proposal, but Rikako didn't mind.

By then, even his lack of assertiveness had become part of what she liked about him. However, she was not the kind of person to decide about marriage on the spot, especially while dining with their boss.

So she said: 'I'll give it good thought and at the right moment, I'd like to give you a proper answer.'

It was a thoroughly Rikako sort of reply, and it brought a smile to Yajima's face.

Her illness was discovered shortly afterwards.

If she told Gaku about it, she could already guess what he would say:

'Even so – if that's what you want, I'd still be happy to marry you.'

There was no way he would take back his proposal just because she was ill. Whether out of kindness or pity, he would go through with it.

But I don't want to see his face contort with sadness as I waste away before his eyes.

And with that weighing on her, before going to the cafe, Rikako had steeled herself.

If I can't be sure I'll still be alive in five years, I won't tell him about the illness. I'll just turn him down.

There would be no need to explain.

'I've thought long and hard about it, but I can't marry you.'

That alone would suffice.

Knowing Gaku's nature, he wouldn't press her for reasons; he would simply say, 'If that's not what you want . . .' and let her go without resistance. That's what she believed.

'Oh, hello there.'

Just as Rikako came to, a woman seated at the counter called out to her.

Looking around, she realized the woman was the only other person in the cafe. She appeared to be in her mid-forties and wore light, sporty clothes – as if she'd been out for a jog or a walk in the neighbourhood, with a small crossbody bag still slung over her shoulder. She was sipping an iced coffee.

'Haven't seen you around lately. What's the deal – did you come from the future?'

'Ah, um, yes.'

Rikako replied instinctively, her intuition telling her that this woman was likely one of the regulars she'd grown close to during the past five years. The woman's words – *haven't seen you around lately* – replayed in her head.

She took a deep breath.

It's OK. I'm not as shocked as I thought I'd be.

She looked down at her hands.

They're not trembling.

Her heartbeat was slightly elevated, but still within a normal range, which gave her a sense of relief.

Good. I'd been worrying about all sorts of things, but now that I know . . . maybe it's not so hard to accept after all.

Before coming to the cafe, Rikako had been wondering—

Five years from now, how will I find out whether I'm still alive?

There was no point in leaping into the future without a plan. If she asked someone who'd never even heard of her, 'Am I still alive?', the best she could expect was a shrug and a 'No idea.'

To be certain of her own fate, she needed people to remember her name and face. That was why she had decided to become a regular at this cafe. Over the next five years, she would make a point of showing up at least once a month to make it known that a woman named Rikako Kabe made regular visits all the way from Yamanashi. The more often she came, the more reliable that impression would be. She was prepared to devote all of her days off to that purpose.

In other words, the fact that this unfamiliar woman had spoken to her meant that her plan to become a regular had more or less succeeded.

Still, that's not a guarantee – this woman might not be one of the regulars who comes every day. Even if I used every day off I had, I could only manage four visits a month. Some months, maybe just two. If the days I came didn't overlap with hers, then, of course, to her, I'd seem like someone she hadn't seen in a while.

Rikako twisted in her seat, stretching her spine to the very edge of leaving it, and craned her neck to get a peek at the far end of the kitchen.

Watching her movements, the woman asked, 'Who did you come to see?'

'Ah, um . . .' Rikako paused briefly before replying. 'Either the owner . . . or the other one – the waitress . . .'

'The other one? You mean Kazu?'

'Ah, y-yes.'

It was at that moment that Rikako first learned Kazu's name.

'Nagare went to Miki's school today – the parents were invited to observe the class – so I don't think he'll be back for a while.'

Rikako didn't know who Miki was, but she nodded as if she did. 'I see.'

Nagare must be the owner . . . So he's not here . . .

'What about Kazu, then?'

'Kazu? Now that you mention it, she stepped out a little while ago . . . I wonder where she went . . .'

'I see . . .'

As she answered, Rikako realized she felt relieved. Her palms were damp with sweat.

So I really am afraid to know the truth. In that case . . . maybe it's OK to leave without learning anything. I'll give up on marrying him. I can't imagine finding happiness in marriage when I don't even know if I'm alive five years from now, not with my feelings this unresolved.

She reached for the cup in front of her.

But it wasn't for nothing. It hurts . . . but at least I've made up my mind to let him go. She sighed quietly.

'Well then, I'll be going . . .'

She gave the woman a polite nod and reached for her cup.

'Oh? Really? Are you sure?'

'Yes. It wasn't anything important . . .'

When Rikako replied, the woman – apparently not all that interested in her – made no effort to stop her. She raised the cup to her lips.

Oh . . .

Though Yaeko had said the coffee would be lukewarm, it was surprisingly hot the moment it touched her lips – far too hot to gulp down in one go. A rich, toasty aroma tickled her nose.

This is what I get for being sensitive to heat.

She gently set the cup back onto the saucer after a single sip.

CLANG-DONG

The entrance bell rang, and Rikako's heart skipped a beat.

N-now? At this moment? Who—?

She turned instinctively towards the entrance, her heart pounding, silently praying that whoever had just walked in wouldn't recognize her.

There are times in life when if one braces for the impact,

injury can be avoided. The bell, however, had rung just at the moment Rikako had decided to flee, and having let her guard down, a shock now would surely hurt her.

The person who entered was Kazu.

'Ah . . .'

The instant Rikako saw her, it was as though she was frozen in place. She couldn't tear her eyes away.

It was less than a second – barely the span of a blink. And yet, for Rikako, it felt like a moment that could decide life or death.

But in stark contrast to the tension gripping Rikako, Kazu appeared calm and casual. She greeted Rikako pleasantly upon spotting her in the time-travel seat.

'Hello. Welcome.'

She nodded politely to the woman at the counter as well, then went into the kitchen.

What . . .?

Kazu's reaction was not at all what Rikako had expected.

Could it be . . .?

Her heart began to race, as if it had suddenly leapt into motion.

Am I . . . still alive?

The possibility struck her like a miracle. She clamped both hands over her mouth, gripped by the urge to shout, *I did it!* at the top of her lungs.

No – wait! It's too soon to celebrate. Maybe . . . maybe she just doesn't know I died.

Trying to calm her rising emotions, Rikako closed her eyes and took a slow, deep breath.

Just then, Kazu returned from the kitchen and spoke to her.

'You came for the timetable, right?'

'What?'

For a moment, Rikako didn't understand what she'd just been asked. Then it hit her – it was the fake reason she had given in order to travel to the future.

'Ah, yes.'

Kazu turned to go to the back room and Rikako tilted her head slightly as she watched her.

Is that the same person who poured my coffee?

Five years ago, Kazu had worn her hair semi-long. Now she had a short bob. She looked different. But that wasn't all. Back then, Kazu had given off the impression of a deep blue ocean, cool and quiet, but the woman she'd just seen now felt more like a pale, translucent blue near the surface – cool to the touch at first, but pleasantly refreshing, like wading in shallow water.

Am I imagining this? No . . . something's changed . . .

It wasn't that her expression had brightened, or that her voice had become more animated.

I don't quite know how to put it . . . but she's definitely not the same as she was five years ago. What could have happened to her?

As Rikako kept her gaze fixed on the doorway to the back room, a sudden sound broke the quiet: a baby's cry. Rikako's eyes widened.

'Oh, she's woken up,' murmured the woman at the counter.

A few minutes later, Kazu returned to the cafe with a timetable in her hand. Just behind her came a man carrying a crying baby. From the way he held the child – calm, practised, tender – Rikako guessed he was Kazu's husband, and that the baby was theirs.

'Koku, you're here?' the woman at the counter called out.

So his name is Koku.

'Yes. I got back yesterday, and tomorrow I'm off abroad again . . .' Koku replied with a wry smile, glancing down at the baby in his arms. Though the woman had posed the question, the way he looked at the baby made it seem as if he was apologizing to her instead.

From behind the counter, Koku bowed politely in Rikako's direction.

'Sorry about this.'

Rikako didn't feel put out, but the baby's cries echoed sharply through the small cafe, loud enough to drown out most of what he'd said.

'It's no problem,' she replied, and at that moment, Kazu stepped forward and handed her the timetable.

'Is this the one you were hoping for?'

Printed on the cover were the words *May 2024 Edition*.

It was, without doubt, a timetable from five years in the future.

'Yes, that's it. Thank you.'

Rikako spoke with a hint of bewilderment on her face. Without opening it to check the contents, she set the timetable down on her lap, then looked at Kazu, and at Koku, holding the baby in his arms.

The woman at the counter turned to Koku.

'Koku, you're starting to look more and more like a proper dad, you know?'

Koku smiled sheepishly. 'I only get to hold her a few times a year. Do I even have the right to call myself a dad?' He looked down at the baby's face.

'You're fine. You don't need qualifications to be a dad. As long as you've got love, that's enough.' She laughed brightly as she said it – light and carefree.

Koku understood what she meant and quickly replied, 'Then I guess I'm good,' breaking into a smile of his own.

He was that kind of person – genuine and open-hearted.

Kazu didn't react; she simply went on with her work in quiet composure.

She likely understood what Koku meant, agreed with the woman's sentiment, and appreciated her for voicing it. And yet, she said nothing – neither confirming nor denying – simply accepting it all as it was. Watching the baby, now asleep and breathing softly in Koku's arms, Kazu allowed herself a faint smile.

Seeing that smile, Rikako thought:

She's happy now.

And then:

I envy her.

The chime of the pendulum wall clock echoed through the cafe, marking the 8 p.m. closing time.

'Oh, it's that late already?'

The woman at the counter jumped up in a panic, paid her bill, and called out cheerfully, 'Well then, Kazu, Koku – see you next time!' before heading out of the door.

After giving Rikako a silent nod, Koku, too, made his exit, slipping quietly into the back room to put his baby to bed.

The cafe fell silent. Now alone with Kazu, Rikako felt the pounding of her heart as if it was shaking her entire body. She felt possessed by the urge to drain her coffee and return to the past that very moment.

I want to know . . .

(But you don't want to know, do you? You're afraid of what you'll hear.)

If closing time had been just ten minutes later – if the woman had lingered, if Koku had still been gently soothing his wakeful child – Rikako would no doubt have finished her coffee and gone back.

Because right now, she was clinging to the hope that she was still alive five years in her future. Kazu's demeanour hadn't struck her as that of someone looking at a deceased former regular.

The five-year survival rate is sixty per cent. I was one of the sixty.

(You just want to believe that. Maybe you should go home with that hope intact.)

But I should ask.

(Even if you do, how do you know she'll tell the truth?)

I should ask, 'Am I still alive?' right here, right now.

(If you said that all of a sudden, you'd probably just confuse her.)

Rikako reached for her cup.

(. . .)

And yet, no matter what the voice in her head told her, she couldn't bring the cup to her lips.

Am I really going to leave without knowing?

She followed Kazu with her eyes as she stepped into the kitchen to begin closing up. Even now, with just the two of them left in the cafe, Kazu's demeanour remained unchanged. There was no sign she was curious why Rikako had come to the future.

Her attitude seemed to say she didn't pry into other people's affairs. And that, somehow, made it all the more frustrating.

If only . . . if only she would say something, anything, simply ask her if something is wrong.

Then perhaps she would be able to confess, without reservation, that she had come to find out whether she was still alive.

But Kazu said nothing.

Unless I ask, she'll never say a word.

(Exactly. So what are you going to do?)

She let her hand fall away from the cup and dropped her gaze to the timetable resting on her lap. On the cover was a photo of a train she had never seen before – a quiet but unmistakable reminder that she had truly come five years into the future.

But I've been coming to this cafe for the past five years. That much is certain. If I were to find out now that I'd died . . . would I really have kept coming here anyway?

(. . .)

No – there's no way. I must have kept coming as a way to let me know I was still alive.

Her thoughts spiralled on.

What other reason would I have had to keep showing up here? I don't know any more. The me from the future – what did she want me to learn? That I lived? Or . . . that I died . . .?

Rikako stared at her hands. The warmth of the cup she'd held earlier came back to her. It would be just the right temperature now for someone like her, who couldn't handle hot drinks. She could probably finish it in one gulp. There wasn't much time left to think.

If I find out, what then?

(If you hear you're already dead . . . could you bear it?)

Why did I come here?

(You made up your mind once already, didn't you?)

Perhaps there are things in life I'm better off not knowing about.

(Yes, give it up. Just go back like this . . .)

But . . . will I regret it?

(. . .)

Can I really say I won't regret leaving without asking? Aren't I just turning away from my own feelings – trying to fool myself?

(But . . .)

It's OK. I've come this far. The only thing left is to trust myself.

(. . . I guess we're right about that.)

At last, the two sides of her – one that wanted to know the

truth, and the other that didn't – came into agreement. Rikako closed her eyes, let out a small breath, then turned her whole body towards the kitchen where Kazu stood.

'Excuse me.'

Kazu appeared almost instantly, as if she had been waiting to be called.

'Yes?'

'There's just one thing I'd like to ask.'

'What is it?' Kazu asked her softly, her kind eyes fixed on Rikako's.

Rikako felt certain that no matter what she asked, Kazu would answer truthfully – with nothing but the plain facts.

'What I want to ask is . . .'

'Yes?'

'. . . Am I . . . am I still . . .'

She faltered.

Her tongue, her lips – everything was prepared to say the word 'alive'. And yet the breath she needed caught in her throat. She didn't know whether it was her own will holding her back, or something else entirely. Unable to bear the tightness in her chest, she drew in shallow breaths, then, forcing the words out, she asked:

'Do I still buy this?'

She lifted the timetable in her hands for Kazu to see.

She had always purchased a copy every month without fail.

If I'm still alive, then I would still be buying it. Which means . . .

She waited for Kazu's reply.

But without pause or hesitation, Kazu answered:

'No. I heard that one would be the last.'

There was not a second's delay, no hint of doubt in her voice.

'I see.'

'Yes.'

There was no regret in Kazu's expression. Just as Rikako had imagined, Kazu conveyed the truth without softening it, without embellishment. Finally, Rikako had got closure. Despite it being everything she had feared, the relief was joyous.

'Thank you. I'm glad it was you I could ask,' she said, meaning it deeply.

The coffee was lukewarm – just right for her. She lifted the cup and drank it down in one long swallow.

After a brief moment, a wave of dizziness washed over her, and the world around her began to shimmer and sway. Her body felt lighter. And then, just like when she had come, it began to dissolve into steam. In that vaporous form, she gave Kazu one last bow.

She saw Kazu looking up at her and then the scene began to slide slowly downward, as if the whole world were tilting gently beneath her. Just before her consciousness slipped away, she saw Kazu lower her head in return, with quiet, deliberate grace.

'Move.'

As the woman in the white dress spoke to her, Rikako realized she had returned from the future.

'S-sorry,' she stammered, hastily rising to give up her seat. In a daze, she stood there, replaying in her mind everything she had just experienced, until Kazu appeared from the kitchen. Handing a fresh cup of coffee to the woman in the white dress, she turned to Rikako and asked: 'Were you able to get the timetable?'

Rikako seemed to have forgotten she was even holding it.

'What? Oh . . . yes, I got it,' she replied. Then as she looked up at Kazu she thought, *No . . . it's not the same. There's a wall between us now.*

She felt an odd sensation – as if the Kazu she had met in the future was a completely different person.

Can someone really seem so changed in just five years?

The realization hit her all over again: she had truly been to the future.

'Do you wish to pay now?' Kazu's voice broke into her thoughts. Rikako had just been to the future. She had got the timetable. There was nothing more to do. Everything she had needed to know, she now knew. There was no reason to stay.

No point in lingering.

Rikako checked the time. It was just about to turn 10 p.m. She paid her bill and left the cafe. Back at street level, the night breeze felt pleasant against her cheek. During the daytime, the warmth had brought a light sweat, but unusually for May, there was a night chill.

I wanted to be sure I'll survive. Without that, I can't say yes.

Rikako opened her text messages on her phone. She scrolled through her history, searching for Gaku's name. Only now did she realize – since the moment he had proposed, she hadn't contacted him once.

She felt a flicker of exasperation that he hadn't followed up either, but then thought, *That's just like him.* He was the kind of person who would wait – wait endlessly – until she reached out. She had always liked that about him. Precisely because of that, she didn't want to leave things vague. She wanted to turn him down properly.

I can't let him keep waiting. I want him to give up on me soon and find happiness with someone else.

She opened the reply window addressed to Gaku, typed, *Can we meet tomorrow?* and sent it with a tap.

'This is the right thing.'

Rikako murmured the words as if to convince herself.

When Rikako awoke the next morning there was just an hour before checkout. She hadn't had a proper night's sleep in weeks. Yet now, knowing what her future held had strangely worked in her favour. It would be a lie to say it didn't hurt. But agonizing over it wouldn't change what lay ahead – what mattered now was how she would live the time she had left. That was how she had begun to see things.

Come to think of it . . .

She checked her messages. There, sent just after 2 a.m., was a reply from Gaku: 'OK.'

Their messages had always been brief, but this response

from Gaku was especially curt. From his point of view, he'd proposed to her – and then she hadn't contacted him even once. He must have been anxious.

Maybe he thinks I'm going to break up with him, Rikako thought. And then, *That might actually make it easier to bring it up*, she decided, letting herself take comfort in the assumption.

She checked out of the hotel, and before heading back to Yamanashi she made a point of reserving a table at the restaurant where she would meet Gaku. The place was a favourite of theirs – a Polish restaurant called Ibasho.

Polish cuisine is rare in Japan. Among its signature dishes is pierogi, dumpling-like wheat-flour parcels filled with ingredients such as meat, potato, spinach, or mushrooms, and boiled or pan-fried. With their chewy texture, pierogi are a hit with Japanese tourists visiting Poland. Other notable dishes include bigos, a sauerkraut and sausage stew; śledź po japońsku, which literally means 'herring in Japanese style'; and placki, pancakes made with a mix of potato and flour. On the streets, one might find pączki, deep-fried doughnuts filled with jam, a beloved dessert among Poles. Rikako and Gaku had fallen under the spell of Polish cuisine at this very restaurant.

Ibasho had a modern, calming atmosphere, with warm, wooden tables and chairs that lent the space a sense of comfort. Soft, indirect lighting bathed the room, and there were private booths – not fully enclosed by doors, but partitioned by walls to create cosy, secluded spaces where one needn't worry about the gaze of other diners. Rikako thought it was the perfect setting for a parting conversation.

She arrived a little later than they had arranged, but Gaku hadn't yet shown up either. It was unusual for him to be late.

That's odd . . . He always lets me know when he's running late . . . As do I, normally . . . For a moment, she wondered if she had got the time wrong, and checked her phone.

It struck her that she had failed to message him that she would be late.

Maybe . . . some part of me doesn't want Gaku to show up. And maybe . . . he's already caught on that I'm going to break things off. That's probably why he's late.

She found herself wishing time would simply stop. But that wish was quietly broken – by Gaku's arrival.

'Sorry.'

'Oh, no – it's fine. I just got here too,' Rikako replied, reaching for the menu as Gaku took the seat across from her.

'Have you ordered?'

'Not yet.'

They had been to this restaurant many times before and always ordered the same things. Even so, Rikako kept her eyes fixed on the menu.

After a short while, a waitress appeared, dressed in a white polo shirt and a red checked apron. 'Have you decided?'

'Sorry, not yet.'

'In that case, may I bring you something to drink first?'

'Then . . . I'll have the apple nalewka. What about you, Gaku?'

When she looked up, Gaku was still staring at the menu.

'I'll have a ginger ale.'

'You're not drinking?'

Gaku loved alcohol. Half the reason he backpacked around the world was to try the local drinks in each country he visited. That he wasn't ordering any today caught Rikako off guard.

'Well . . . I'm just not in the mood,' he said, with a bitter smile.

Rikako understood at once. *He knows. He knows I'm going to turn his proposal down.*

Suddenly, it felt wrong to be the only one drinking. She turned to the waitress.

'Excuse me, actually – can I change that to orange juice?'

Gaku was still staring at the menu.

He didn't say, 'You should go ahead and drink.'

That wasn't the kind of man he was – he never pushed.

The silence dragged on.

The air is so heavy . . . How am I supposed to bring it up in this atmosphere?

Rikako gazed at the menu again. She had to decide on a dish, but in this state, she couldn't imagine being able to eat a bite.

If possible, she wanted Gaku to be the one to say it – So . . . have you decided about the proposal? – but he kept his eyes glued to the menu.

But if it comes up now and I say no . . . he might just get up and leave before the drinks even arrive. I'll be stuck here alone with orange juice. That would be too embarrassing.

She hated herself for caring about appearances even in a moment like this. Still, she decided to wait until after the meal to bring it up.

She settled on a light salad. Normally, she would've ordered her favourite bigos, and Gaku would be picking at pierogi, savouring a beer, then wine, maybe even some vodka or Spirytus.

Gaku often called himself a bottomless bucket, boasting that no amount of beer or sake could get him drunk. And yet today, not a drop. For both of them, this meal had become an uncomfortable ordeal.

Gaku must be hurting too.

Unable to bear the silence any longer, Rikako put her fork down, feeling guilty that she'd hardly touched her salad. Taking a deep breath, careful not to let Gaku notice, she finally spoke.

'Um . . .' Then she paused, preparing herself to say, 'About your proposal . . .' and looked up.

'Here.'

Gaku slid a small navy-blue box towards her.

'I didn't get the chance to give this to you when I proposed before.' He said it with a shy smile.

'What?'

Rikako was thrown completely off balance.

Wait – what's going on? Didn't Gaku realize I was going to turn him down?

While they were out of contact, Gaku was regretting the way he had proposed to Rikako on the spur of the moment. If he was going to propose, he wished he had at least prepared a ring. More than anything, what weighed on him was how lacking in resolve his words had sounded.

Rikako had thought the proposal was just like him – but in truth, he hadn't simply been trying to put her feelings first.

Gaku did not lack initiative, but he felt overwhelming stress at the thought of his actions inconveniencing others. It led him to suppress his own thoughts and emotions.

Say someone invited him to dinner and asked, 'What do you feel like eating?' If he replied, 'Ramen,' and the other person responded with a hesitant, 'Ramen, huh?' Gaku would immediately assume that the mismatch in preferences had made the other person uncomfortable – and he'd feel stressed.

What he couldn't stand was rejection. So if he was craving ramen, noodle soup, but the other person wanted yakiniku, grilled meat, he'd go along with that, even if he didn't like it. The stress of eating something he disliked was more bearable than the stress of being turned down. This tendency was especially strong around people close to him: friends, family, his parents. And so he came to be seen as lacking in initiative, someone who would simply go with the flow.

When he was a student he had travelled the world alone, not because he was aimless, but because travelling solo meant he didn't have to worry about others and could choose where to go. In other words, it wasn't that he lacked opinions or a will of his own. He had his own wishes – he knew exactly what he wanted.

'I'd like to marry you . . . if that's what you want.'

That was how he'd proposed to Rikako. And Rikako, taking his words at face value, thought: *If I want to marry him, he's willing to go through with it. But if I say no, then it's not something he'll fight for. It's not something he wants badly enough to push for.*

But the truth was, Gaku had been thinking: *I want to marry Rikako.*

That was why he never imagined she would turn down his proposal.

Meanwhile, Rikako had interpreted his lateness as hesitation. *He must be afraid I'm going to reject him, and now he's avoiding me,* she thought.

But in reality, Gaku had done what he always did – he'd sent a message saying, 'I'll be a little late.' It was just bad luck that the signal was poor and the message never went through.

As for why Gaku, a lover of alcohol, had ordered ginger ale – it was simply because he didn't want to be tipsy on such an important day, the day he planned to give her a ring.

Even the silence between them had its own explanation. Gaku was never one to chatter. He was the type to simply listen, nodding and saying, 'Mm-hmm, mm-hmm,' as Rikako talked. So naturally, if she didn't speak, silence would follow. But silence didn't bother him. What mattered to him was being with Rikako.

That said, he was a little nervous that day too. He wasn't sure when would be the right moment to hand her the ring.

That one thought kept circling in his head, making him even quieter than usual. As much as five whole minutes had passed since the food was served, and, still, not one word had been spoken by either of them. For Rikako, who had just seen her own future and was preparing to decline his proposal, those five minutes felt like thirty – or an hour. But for Gaku, it was just five ordinary minutes.

Their sense of time had diverged completely, each warped by the state of their own heart.

'The size is the one you told me last year . . . but if it doesn't fit, they said it can be resized,' Gaku murmured, averting his gaze as if embarrassed, speaking more to himself than to her.

'Wait a second. Listen—'

'Sorry . . . about everything.'

'What?'

Suddenly, Gaku bowed his head. Rikako was unsure what was happening.

'What? Why are you apologizing?'

'Yajima told me . . . that the way I proposed to you was all wrong . . .'

'What do you mean?'

Rikako couldn't understand what was supposed to be wrong about it. To her, it had felt like a very *Gaku* kind of proposal.

'I said, "If that's what you want," but Yajima, when I told him, called me out on it. He asked me what I'd do if you said you didn't want to get married – would I just give up? He said there was no feeling behind my proposal. That I needed to express my own feelings first, that if I want to make you happy, I should tell you that. He said the way I proposed sounded like I was saying, from the start, that even if you end up unhappy, that's your decision, so it's not my responsibility.'

Yajima didn't truly believe Gaku felt that way deep down. What he meant was that Gaku needed to communicate his feelings more clearly, without leaving room for misunderstandings. Having taken Yajima's advice to heart, Gaku's intention today was to propose again, but properly this time.

I had no idea there'd been a conversation like that between him and Yajima . . . but still . . . It was painful, but she had already decided what to say when turning him down: *Though I'm grateful for your feelings, Gaku, I simply can't picture a happy future for the two of us.*

The candle in the middle of the table flickered, and the soft strains of live piano music flowed quietly through the room.

Gaku took a deep breath and picked up the ring box from the table.

Ah . . .

Rikako noticed that his hand was trembling.

Gaku?

She lifted her face to look at him, and just as their eyes met, Gaku slowly opened the lid. Inside, a diamond ring sat nestled in velvet, catching the candlelight and glittering like the sea at sunset.

'I think . . . maybe I said, "If that's what you want," because I was afraid. Afraid you'd say no if I told you how I really felt.'

I see.

'I don't know what's troubling you right now . . . but I can tell from your face – you're planning to turn me down.'

He knows . . .

'Even so, I don't want to give up on marrying you. I won't give up.'

His voice was unsteady and his words came haltingly. But to Rikako, they rang unmistakably true. This wasn't a polished proposal. It wasn't graceful. But it was honest. It reached her heart.

'So,' Gaku continued, 'will you marry me?'

Tears welled in Rikako's eyes and rolled down her cheeks.

Now I know. I've been afraid too. Afraid to tell him I'm ill. Afraid that he'd regret proposing if he knew. That he'd say he couldn't marry someone who might die soon. So, I tried to run away. I thought if I turned him down first, I wouldn't get hurt.

'Gaku, I . . .'

She covered her face with both hands and wept, unable to stop the flow of tears.

All lives come to an end some day. Yaeko lost her sister in an accident, and she still lives with strength. I thought I was protecting Gaku from the sorrow of losing me some day. I thought it would be too cruel to let him be happy for only a little while, then make him have to let go. I decided for him that he'd be better off without me. But . . .

A vision of Kazu Tokita from the future flickered through her mind – of Kazu watching the moment when Koku held his baby with a look of pure happiness. Rikako remembered how much she had envied that.

Even so, I want to be happy. With this man.

Rikako lifted her tear-streaked face and looked into Gaku's eyes.

Is there anyone else who could make me this happy? No . . . there isn't.

She covered her face again with trembling hands.

'Ri . . . Rikako?'

'I'm sorry. I'm sorry, Gaku.'

The words were on the tip of her tongue. But she couldn't quite say them.

'I also . . .'

I want to be happy with you. But I'm scared. I don't know if I can take responsibility for those words.

The soft notes of the piano continued in the quiet restaurant. Rikako couldn't stop crying.

Gaku stood up and knelt beside her.

Then he said:

'I understand. I can tell just by looking at you. I will *absolutely* make you happy.'

He took her hand.

'So I'll say it again, OK?'

'OK.'

'Will you marry me?'

Gaku took out the ring and held it out to her.

'Gaku . . .'

Rikako stared at the ring finger of her left hand.

If it's him . . . I can tell him everything. Even about my illness. And I know – he'll still make me happy. We'll be happy. Right until the very end, we'll be happy. I believe that. So, as long as I'm alive, I won't give up. Not on happiness. Not with him.

She gave him a small nod, offered him her left hand, and – smiling through her tears – said: 'Yes.'

Late April 2024

A few days before Rikako would come from the past, Gaku visited the cafe to leave a timetable for her. Seated at a table, he was quietly jotting down a note.

'That baby of yours never cries, does he?'

Fumiko Kiyokawa, holding an infant at the counter seat, sounded surprised. The baby lay in her arms, smiling contentedly.

'No, he doesn't. He even sleeps through the night, which has been a real help,' Gaku replied, slipping his note into the pages of the timetable.

At times, Gaku had accompanied Rikako on her regular visits to the cafe and he had got to know Fumiko. Not only was she also a regular, but lately, when Kazu was away at Kinuyo Mita's painting class, she helped out behind the counter.

'Lucky you. I want a baby too – soon.'

'Where's Goro these days?'

'Germany.'

Goro was Fumiko's fiancé. They'd once worked together, but now he was employed at a major video game company, earning a name for himself.

'It sounds like he is doing really well.'

'Yeah, he is.'

Fumiko's face, as she answered, showed a quiet mix of pride and loneliness – the joy of seeing Goro thrive doing what he loved, tinged with the sadness of not being by his side.

'All right, I'll leave this with you,' Gaku said, standing up and handing the timetable across the counter to Kazu, while stealing a glance at Fumiko, who still looked a little down.

Kazu took the timetable and stared at it.

'Leave it with us,' she replied, though her expression seemed to ask: *Is that all? Shouldn't there be a message or something?*

Gaku hesitated for a moment, then smiled.

'I slipped a message inside. I don't know if my wife will ever read it, though.'

'You didn't ask?' Fumiko interjected.

'Ask what?'

'Whether Rikako actually read your message . . .'

At that, Gaku chuckled softly.

'No, I only just wrote it on the spur of the moment. Until today, I hadn't even thought of putting a message in the timetable.'

'Oh . . . right!'

Fumiko stuck out her tongue in mock-exasperation at her own silly question.

Suddenly, the pendulum wall clock chimed, and the baby in Fumiko's arms flinched, then began to fuss. Fumiko tried to soothe the child, but it was no use – the baby burst into tears.

'Oh dear . . .'

'Well, we should be going . . .'

Gaku stepped in, gently taking the baby from Fumiko's arms.

'This will be the last time I buy a timetable,' he said with a small smile. 'I'm not the type to enjoy imaginary journeys through train schedules . . .'

With practised hands, he slipped the baby into the carrier across his chest.

'Thanks for taking care of that,' he added, bowing once again toward Kazu.

Kazu, looking down, gave a little nod in reply.

'Gaku,' Fumiko called out, just as he turned to leave.

'Yes?'

'Um . . . this might be a rude thing to ask, but I just couldn't stop thinking about it . . .'

'You mean the message?'

'Ah . . . yes. I'm a little curious . . .'

What Gaku had written was a letter addressed to his late wife. And whether Rikako had ever seen it – he didn't know.

If Rikako never noticed it, then wouldn't Gaku's feelings just . . . go, unseen?

Fumiko had said it was a tactless question, but deep down, she had simply wanted there to be someone who knew how much Gaku had loved Rikako. She knew she had no real right to ask, but she couldn't stay silent.

'I'm sorry . . . I know it was a message for Rikako . . .' she said, bowing her head in apology.

Gaku understood what she meant. And he was touched.

Maybe . . . if someone knows what I wrote – knows how I felt – then some part of me and Rikako, some proof that we lived, might live on in their heart.

Scratching his head shyly, Gaku murmured, 'It's nothing much, really . . . but if you'd like, after I'm gone . . . go ahead and read it.'

With that, he left the cafe.

CLANG-DONG

A quiet sob escaped Fumiko as she read the message.

You never gave up – not until the very end.
And right up to the end, you looked so happy.
Thank you.
From your loving husband and son.

IV

The Father and Son

Late October 2019

'My dream?'

Nagare Tokita, the owner of the cafe Funiculi Funicula, tilted his head and folded his arms as he thought. He was responding to a question posed by Kinuyo Mita, a regular. Kinuyo ran her own small art school. She specialized in watercolours and had once illustrated the cover of a well-known novel. She had even published an art book of her own. But that was more than thirty years ago. In recent years, she had dedicated herself to nurturing young, aspiring artists.

The question she had asked Nagare was: 'What's your dream?'

Nagare was thinking in silence, so Kinuyo turned the question to Koku Shintani, who was seated at the table near the entrance. He had been a year ahead of Kazu Tokita at the art university she had attended and now travelled the world photographing ruins.

'Then how about you, Koku? What's your dream?'

He replied without hesitation. 'Me? My dream is to marry Kazu.'

Kazu was in the cafe too, and of course she heard him, but she treated the remark as if it had nothing to do with her.

Kinuyo, though, smiled and looked at her.

'It's lovely, isn't it? The way he can say that with no hesitation, even in front of you.'

Kazu didn't object. She just replied, 'Yes, I suppose.'

'I've already been turned down once, but I'm not giving up.'

'Even better.' Kinuyo clapped lightly in admiration at Koku's response. She had long hoped someone like Koku, steadfast and sure of his feelings, would appear before Kazu. 'I'm cheering you on.'

'I'll do my best.'

While the two chatted, Kazu quietly continued wrapping paper napkins around spoons. Her expression showed neither embarrassment nor awkwardness.

Beside her stood Nagare, his arms still folded, gazing up at the ceiling.

'So? What about your dream, Nagare?' Kinuyo asked again, her expression suggesting: *You've had plenty of time to think.*

Even then, he didn't answer right away. He let out a thoughtful 'Hmm . . .' before saying, 'Maybe . . . hearing people say what I serve is good?'

Kinuyo blinked at his answer, the product of such intense deliberation.

'But that's already come true, hasn't it? Your coffee's delicious – honestly, to me, it's the best in the world. If someone asked me, "What do you want before you die?" I'd say, "Nagare's coffee," without hesitation.'

That was how much Kinuyo loved what Nagare brewed.

'You're right. I guess my dream already came true.' He narrowed his eyes even further – a tell-tale sign he was happy.

Noticing his expression, Kinuyo exclaimed, 'Isn't that wonderful.' She nodded in satisfaction.

'So then, what's *your* dream, Kinuyo?' Nagare asked.

In his mind, he was already anticipating her answer: to train a top-tier artist, to hold another solo exhibition, to publish a new art collection – something related to painting.

He didn't know much about art. But he remembered his impression upon seeing Kinuyo's work for the first time.

It calms me. I could look at it for hours. It feels . . . somehow nostalgic.

His mother, Yukari, who had since moved to Hakodate and was now running a cafe called Donna Donna, pouring the coffee that whisks customers away to the past or future, had said, 'Kinuyo's paintings will absolutely go up in value one day. I'm sure of it.' She had even purchased a few.

In fact, the paintings Kinuyo created before retiring and opening her art school had already started fetching high prices. Some sold for several million yen. So naturally, Nagare had assumed Kinuyo's dream was something to do with art.

But it wasn't.

'My dream,' she said with a gentle smile towards Kazu, 'is for Kazu to be happy. That's all.'

At Kinuyo's words, Kazu's hands stilled. She kept her eyes lowered and, without a word, offered only the slightest of bows. She appreciated the sentiment, but she couldn't live up to that hope. Her expression made that plain.

Watching the two of them stirred up a mixture of feelings in Nagare.

When Kazu was seven, she had poured the coffee for her mother, Kaname Tokita, so she could return to the past to see her late husband one last time. But she never came back. She did not finish drinking the coffee before it went cold, and why she failed to do so remained a mystery. Because of the cafe's rule, she became a ghost, bound to the seat for time travel. From that day on, Kazu felt responsible, and stopped thinking about her own happiness.

Only Nagare and Kinuyo knew the full story of what had happened. So for Nagare, Kinuyo's wish for Kazu to be happy – despite her knowing the reason for her not to be – felt deeply precious.

CLANG-DONG

'H-hello. Welcome!' Nagare called out in response to the bell at the entrance.

A boy who looked to be in junior high school stepped through the door. He wore a navy three-quarter coat, his two-block haircut was neatly styled, and he carried himself with quiet composure. He was even shorter than Kazu, who was already on the small side. Nagare wondered if he might actually still be in elementary school.

'Is it just you?' Nagare asked.

He thought the boy looked a little tense, though whether that was because he intended to sit in the time-travelling seat or because he was intimidated by someone of Nagare's towering size was unclear. Either way, Nagare decided to speak to him in a friendly tone, hoping to put him at ease.

'Yes, I'm alone.'

'Mind if I ask your name?'

'Yeah, sure. I'm Tsuguo Suga.'

Tsuguo took off his coat and sat at a table in the middle of the cafe.

'How old are you, Tsuguo?' asked Kinuyo, joining the conversation.

'Fourteen.'

'Second year of junior high?'

'Yes.'

'You're very composed. Polite too. And the way you carry yourself, it's mature.'

'Thank you.'

'Isn't he, though?'

Kinuyo glanced at Nagare, as if seeking agreement in her assessment of the boy as polite and unusually grown-up.

'He sure is,' Nagare said. He'd been thinking the same thing.

'What can I get you?'

Kazu emerged from behind the counter to take his order, timing her approach exactly at a lull in the conversation between Kinuyo and the boy. But when Tsuguo looked at the menu she handed him, his face fell.

'Um . . .'

Apparently, the item he was hoping for wasn't listed.

Kinuyo quickly picked up on his disappointment.

'The owner here will make something for you even if it's not on the menu, you know,' she said gently.

'Really?'

'Isn't that right?' she added, directing her gaze towards Nagare.

'Anything you like,' he replied with a theatrical bow, placing a hand on his chest.

Tsuguo looked slightly startled, but upon hearing he could order what he liked, he relaxed a little.

'Then . . . could I have carbonara?'

'Carbonara. Got it. And a drink?'

'Um . . .' Tsuguo thought for a moment. 'Just the carbonara is fine. And could I have some water?'

'Sure thing.'

Nagare scribbled *carbonara* on the order slip and hurried to the kitchen.

'You like carbonara?' Kinuyo asked. She seemed charmed by his exceptionally good manners for a boy of his age.

'Yeah. My dad used to make it a lot.'

'I see.' The past tense didn't escape her notice, nor did the way his expression clouded slightly.

He might have passed . . .

It was rare for a fourteen-year-old to visit this cafe without a reason. Kinuyo wondered if Tsuguo had come to meet a father he could no longer see.

But it wasn't something to pry into lightly.

'The one Nagare makes is delicious,' she offered instead.

'I'm looking forward to it,' Tsuguo replied with a smile.

'Well, I'll be off now.' Suddenly, Koku Shintani rose from the table near the entrance.

'Oh? Heading out already?' Kinuyo looked over from the counter, still holding her half-drunk coffee.

Koku held the bill and reached for the bag on the seat opposite – inside was the camera gear he used for work.

'I'm leaving for France tomorrow.'

'More ruins?'

'Yes.'

'Don't you have any interest in people, Koku?'

Koku specialized in landscape photography and had published several photo books featuring ruins. None of his photographs included people, and the jobs he accepted were always for landscape photography. Kinuyo, who specialized in portraits, didn't actually believe he lacked interest in people, but she was curious why he chose ruins as his subject.

'No, it's not that,' he answered. 'I like capturing ruins because they hold the echoes of where people once lived. They make me think about who those people were, how they lived.

In fact, I think I'm more interested in people than anyone. You know, I often think my photos might be the opposite of Kazu's paintings. Kazu never paints people, but that's what makes her work so intriguing. I really love that about her art.'

As he spoke, he looked at Kazu. He was thinking of the painting she had made in university, which depicted a familiar, lived-in streetscape, stripped of all human presence. Koku photographed the remnants of human life in places long abandoned; Kazu painted places where people should be part of the scene, yet she refused to let them appear. Though both omitted people, their creative impulses moved in opposite directions: Koku reached towards humanity through absence; Kazu withdrew from it.

Kinuyo, her sensibilities honed by a life in art, also felt that quiet difference. She looked at the two of them, standing on either side of the cash register, and smiled.

'You know, you really do suit each other.'

Kazu let Kinuyo's words slide past her, as though they had nothing to do with her.

'That'll be four hundred and twenty yen for the cream soda,' she said calmly.

'Here.' Koku retrieved the exact amount from his coin pouch and set it clinking on the tray.

'Perfect. Thank you very much.'

Kazu pounded the clunky keys of the register and dropped the coins into the till.

Koku turned and gave Kinuyo a parting bow.

'Good luck,' Kinuyo murmured as she waved him goodbye – not for the work he was about to do in France. It was her way of cheering on the man who, despite Kazu's indifference, never let go of his steadfast affection for her.

CLANG-DONG

Once Koku had left the cafe, Kinuyo leaned over the counter to speak to Kazu.

'He's a good lad,' she murmured with a sincerity echoing what she was really thinking: *Perhaps Koku's the only one who could make Kazu happy.*

'Yes,' Kazu replied. She knew what Kinuyo was getting at, but rather than object, she let it pass. After all, Koku was, in many ways, a *good lad*, so she chose to agree based on her interpretation – not Kinuyo's.

'Sorry for the wait!'

Nagare emerged from the kitchen. He handed a silver tray to Kazu bearing a plate of carbonara and a small salad. The dish apparently had turned out to his liking, judging by his beaming smile.

'Here you are.'

Kazu brought the freshly made meal to Tsuguo. The boy leaned forward and peered down at the plate in front of him.

'Wow . . .'

Tsuguo couldn't help but voice his awe.

'Please, enjoy it while it's hot . . .' Nagare said to Tsuguo, who was still gazing at the carbonara.

'Oh, right.'

Tsuguo hurried to pick up his fork, twirling the pasta carefully at the edge of the plate until he had a bite-sized portion. He brought it to his mouth.

'It's delicious,' he said, breaking into a wide smile.

Seeing that expression, Kinuyo peered up at Nagare and said, 'Another dream come true, wouldn't you say?'

'Looks like it,' Nagare replied, his eyes narrowing with quiet satisfaction.

Tsuguo ate with innocent enthusiasm for a few moments, but his mood suddenly shifted. He sniffled once, then tears began to spill down his cheeks.

Yet no one asked him what was wrong. Nagare, like Kinuyo, sensed that he had come here with a purpose. This cafe wasn't the kind of place a junior-high student stumbled into by chance. That purpose, they both suspected, was to return to the past.

'I'm sorry.'

Once his tears had subsided, Tsuguo reached into his coat pocket and pulled out a small pack of tissues. He wiped his cheeks.

'The carbonara was really good.'

'I'm glad to hear that,' Kinuyo said gently, then glanced towards Nagare, her eyes doing the talking: *Shouldn't we ask?*

Perhaps the boy wasn't entirely sure yet whether this was really *that* cafe. Without that certainty, asking, *'May I return to the past?'* would be daunting. And if that was indeed why he had come, then it fell to the cafe's owner to confirm it.

Nagare had reached the same conclusion. He understood Kinuyo's glance and leaned over the counter to address Tsuguo directly.

'Hey . . . have you ever heard the rumour about this cafe? It says . . . you can travel to the past from here.'

At the word *past*, Tsuguo's eyes widened for a moment in surprise. But when he answered, his tone was calm.

'I've heard about it.'

'So you really did come . . . to go back?' Nagare asked.

'Yes. I want to see my father . . . he passed away.'

'Do you know the rules?'

'More or less, yes.'

'I see . . .'

Tsuguo's composure began to falter and his face clouded over.

'What's wrong?' Kinuyo asked. She had expected the boy to feel relieved now that the rumour was confirmed, but he looked more troubled than before.

'Actually . . .' With his eyes lowered and his voice barely audible, Tsuguo confessed: 'I don't know if my father ever came to this cafe.'

'What?' Kinuyo and Nagare exchanged glances. One of the key rules about returning to the past was this: *you cannot meet someone who has never visited the cafe.* In other words, if Tsuguo's father had never set foot inside this place, then no matter what, the boy would not be able to meet him again. The heavy gloom on his face came from this very fear.

'I read an article online about this cafe . . .'

'An article?' Kinuyo looked to Nagare as if asking, *Have you heard about this?*

'First time I've heard about it,' he replied. Nagare didn't carry a smartphone, nor did he browse the internet on a computer. As it turned out, the article Tsuguo had seen wasn't widely circulated: it was one of those obscure blog posts that surfaced via a random recommendation algorithm. The story was about someone who went back to the past to say a proper goodbye to their beloved dog that had died in the night. Most of the comments under the article dismissed it as fiction, and even those numbered fewer than ten. Considering today's internet saturation, it was safe to say almost no one had read it.

But it had left a deep impression on Tsuguo.

'My parents split up just after I was born, so my dad raised me. He . . . he passed away about four months ago because of his heart condition. It was so sudden . . .'

His found it difficult to speak. But rather than letting his emotions break him, he swallowed the wave rising inside and forced himself to go on. His quiet resilience brought tears to Kinuyo's eyes.

'When I read the article . . . I couldn't sit still. If there was really a way to go back and see my dad again, even just once . . .'

No matter how composed he might seem, Tsuguo was still only fourteen. The grief of losing a parent you depend on doesn't heal in four months. His desire to see his father again, if only for a moment, had simply grown too strong to suppress. Tears burst from his eyes once more, as if a dam had broken. Nagare's eyes thinned to slits as he sniffled quietly. Kinuyo pulled out a handkerchief and dabbed at the corners of her eyes.

'I'm sorry,' Tsuguo said, wiping his faces with a tissue. 'My dad was a chef. I remembered him saying, a few years back, that he'd had a really good carbonara in Jimbocho. The cafe in the article was in Jimbocho, so I thought . . . maybe . . .'

'I see. So that's why,' said Kinuyo. The image of him breaking down in tears while eating the pasta still lingered in her mind. She and Nagare both wanted more than anything to let him meet his father. But there was no certainty, just too many unknowns.

Nagare looked worried and a deep furrow creased his brow.

'Do you know about how long ago that might've been? When he said he had that carbonara in Jimbocho?'

Kinuyo sat down across from Tsuguo, trying to tease out any clue that might help.

'Let me think . . . I was in fourth grade, so I guess it was about four years ago.'

'Four years, I see . . .'

Nagare tried to remember whether they'd served carbonara four years ago. It was around the time Fumiko Kiyokawa and Yaeko Hirai had returned to the past. Back then, Nagare's wife, Kei Tokita, had still been alive – and carbonara had been one of her specialities. He remembered Yaeko's younger sister coming in and Kei preparing her signature chicken and shiso cream pasta. His eyes drifted to her photo near the cash register.

What would she say, if she were here? Kei had been carefree and full of light, a woman who never hesitated to befriend anyone, no matter how unfamiliar. *She'd probably just say, 'Why not give it a try?' without a second thought.*

Nagare gazed down at her smiling face in the photo and thought that her advice had often seemed reckless; yet more often than not, it turned out to be the simplest and most effective path.

I keep worrying about what happens if this boy goes back and can't meet his father. But if Kei were here, she would only think about what happens if he can.

Nagare decided. He said, 'Hey . . . why don't you just give it a try?'

His tone was tentative, as if to say, 'I'm not claiming this is the right answer, but it's what came to mind,' but Kinuyo responded with, 'That was sudden. You sounded just like Kei for a moment.'

'Yeah . . . I thought that's what she'd say if she were here. Maybe he won't be able to see his father. But that wouldn't be a tragedy – just a sign his father had never been to this cafe. Rules are rules, after all. But if he *can* see him, then that's a gift. Which means, if there's even a chance to gain that kind of happiness, why not take it? I think . . . Kei would've seen it that way. Don't you?'

Kinuyo was still surprised by how uncharacteristic Nagare sounded, but she nodded firmly and said, 'Yes, that's true. You're absolutely right.'

Tsuguo, too, perhaps encouraged by Nagare's words, had a sparkle in his eyes. The gloom had vanished.

Thank goodness, Nagare thought as he watched the change in his expression, and let out a quiet breath of relief. He started to clear the plate, then asked, 'Just to be safe, do you mind if we go over the rules one more time?'

'Sure. Let's see. You can't meet someone who's never been to this cafe. You can't change reality. You can't leave the cafe . . . and there's a time limit too, right?'

'You've mostly got it,' Nagare replied. 'Just one clarification though. You're right about not being able to leave the cafe. But that's just a consequence of the rule. The actual rule is that once you sit in the seat to return to the past, you can't get up from it. If you do, you'll be pulled straight back to the present. So remember, if you do get to meet your dad, stay seated. It would be a shame to ruin the moment like that.'

'I see. Got it.'

'And there's one more thing. The most important.'

'What's that?'

'If you go back, be sure to finish the coffee before it gets cold. Understood?'

'Yes, I know. If I don't finish the coffee, I'll become a ghost, right?'

'Yeah . . .'

Nagare was relieved to hear he understood the risk. Still, he felt a flicker of unease. So he fixed Tsuguo with a serious gaze and said, 'Even if you meet your dad – don't forget the coffee.'

'I won't. I understand.'

Tsuguo smiled as he spoke, and in that pure smile was the reflection of the wish to see his father, and the hope that he might be able to.

Two hours had passed since Tsuguo began waiting for the seat that could let him return to the past. Kinuyo had gone home, and Nagare had taken his daughter Miki out shopping. Now, only Kazu Tokita and Tsuguo remained.

Flap.

The sudden snap of a book closing echoed through the quiet cafe. Tsuguo, who had been poring over a study guide for his exams, looked up. The woman in the white dress was rising from her seat.

His gaze followed her as she slowly moved towards him, then he looked to Kazu behind the counter.

If I sit in that seat, I can go back . . . right?

His eyes asked the question, and Kazu replied with a subtle nod before slipping into the kitchen.

The woman in the white dress passed by him, her footsteps inaudible as she made her way to the toilet. Tsuguo was now alone – but he didn't panic. Nagare had already explained what he should do and he understood why Kazu had gone into the kitchen.

He turned to face the chair she had vacated and slowly rose. Gingerly, he approached it, clinging to the hope it would whisk him back to the past. He felt his heartbeat begin to quicken.

Please . . . let me see my father.

He called up memories of the days they had spent together as heat pricked at his closed eyes.

His father in the bedroom each morning, waking to the alarm, preparing his lunchbox, sending him off. Coming home from school to hear 'Welcome back', and when his father was away for work, there was always a delicious dinner waiting. They bathed together, went to amusement parks, to the sea, to the mountains. He could talk to his father about anything; he had loved him like a best friend. And he had never once doubted that life would go on like that for ever.

But the end had come without warning. Tsuguo still remembered the night his father was writhing in agony, clutching his chest, crying out in pain. He remembered standing there watching, unable to control his trembling. He never imagined that would be their final goodbye.

Footsteps approached softly. It was Kazu, carrying a silver tray with a white cup and a small kettle. She looked at Tsuguo, still staring at the chair, and said, 'Please, have a seat.'

'S-sure . . .'

Tsuguo slid carefully into the space between the chair and table, his face solemn.

It feels cold somehow . . .

The chill on his skin told him the space he was in was special. Kazu quietly set the cup in front of him and began the preparations.

'Are you ready? I'll now pour your coffee. You'll return to the past from the moment I pour it, and you'll stay there only until it goes cold.'

'Yes.'

'And you understand what happens if you don't finish it in time?'

'I do.'

It was the first time he was having what you'd call a proper conversation with Kazu. As she gave her instructions in an even, measured tone, Tsuguo felt his heartbeat getting steadily faster.

'One other thing: it's hard to tell exactly when the coffee has fully cooled. So I'll put this in . . .'

She picked up a slender ten-centimetre-long rod from the tray and placed it in the cup. 'It will alert you when the coffee is about to go cold. When it beeps, drink the rest immediately.'

'O – OK. So as soon as it sounds, I finish the coffee?'

'That's right.'

Brushing aside his awe at Kazu's solemn air, Tsuguo thought, *I don't dislike coffee – I'm sure I can finish it.*

'One more thing: visualization. Picture an image of your father here in this cafe.'

'Even if he never actually came?'

'Yes. If the image of him *not* coming is stronger, you could end up returning to when he wasn't here, even if he had come once.'

'Oh . . .'

'Which is why . . .'

'I have to believe he came here. And picture it?'

'Exactly.'

'Got it.'

He closed his eyes and imagined the scene of his father at the cafe. *It's OK. I can picture him being here. It's not that hard.* He opened his eyes and looked at Kazu. *I'm ready*, his gaze said.

The cafe fell silent. Only the ticking of the wall clock echoed, loud and steady.

Dong, dong, dong . . .

The deep chimes rang out, announcing five o'clock.

'Then,' Kazu said, reaching for the silver kettle, 'before the coffee gets cold,' she added in a whisper.

Tsuguo's father was named Ryutaro. He had a heart valve abnormality and had been diagnosed with angina, a condition where the heart's blood flow is temporarily reduced, causing chest pain. While common causes include high blood pressure, high cholesterol, smoking, obesity, and lack of exercise, in Ryutaro's case, his grandfather and great-grandfather had both died from the condition. Doctors suspected genetics, rather than lifestyle, played the stronger role in his illness.

Ryutaro had once told Tsuguo, 'Your mother and I divorced just after you were born.' But the truth was that she had abandoned them. Unable to cope with raising a child, she had disappeared from their lives.

Tsuguo had no idea. Even when, as a young boy, he'd asked, 'Why did you and Mum split up?' Ryutaro would only reply, looking deeply apologetic, 'It must have been my fault.'

Perhaps sensing his father's pain, Tsuguo wanted to reassure him: *'But to me, you're the best dad in the world!'*

From then on, he would say this often, trying to cheer Ryutaro.

He believed that the loneliness he felt without a mother was surely something his father felt too.

That's why he made a vow: *I'll never, ever disappear from Dad's life. No matter what happens.*

That vow, spoken only in his heart, had reached Ryutaro. His son was precious to him beyond words. Ryutaro worked as a chef in a restaurant, and though his hours were irregular, he never went out drinking after work, even when invited by colleagues. He always came straight home. When he came up with new menu ideas, he would often try them at home first and let Tsuguo taste them. Tsuguo loved his father's cooking more than eating out anywhere.

Above all, his favourite dish was carbonara. Whenever Ryutaro heard about a recipe that people praised as exceptional, he would try making it himself to serve to Tsuguo.

One day, Ryutaro ate a carbonara at a certain cafe that stunned him. It was, without question, the best he had ever tasted.

I want Tsuguo to taste this carbonara too.

Ryutaro pictured his son's face, bright with joy, smiling as he said, *'Delicious,'* after taking a bite.

I just have to find out how it's made.

But as a chef himself, he knew well that asking another in the trade for their recipe was frowned upon. In the worst case, it could even lead to a bitter argument. Still, he had already tried several times to recreate the dish on his own, and no matter what he did, he couldn't quite get it right.

He longed so much to hear that simple, heartfelt *'Delicious'* from Tsuguo that he couldn't give up.

A carbonara this good must have some secret – a technique or ingredient no one else knows.

Ryutaro decided to humble himself and bow his head to the cafe's chef, asking if he would share the recipe. He braced himself, already guessing he would refuse: *You think I'd tell you? Get out!* But when the chef appeared, he replied casually, 'Of course.'

To Ryutaro's surprise, he even went so far as to jot the recipe down on a slip of paper and hand it to him.

Ryutaro thanked him over and over before finally leaving the cafe.

When Tsuguo awoke, he found that he was alone with Kazu, who was standing behind the counter.

Have I really gone back to the past?

He looked around, but since the cafe was on the second basement floor, he couldn't tell if it was day or night.

The woman who made my coffee earlier is wearing the same clothes, and there's no calendar in sight . . .

'Um, may I ask you something?' he said politely, addressing Kazu.

'Yes,' she replied quietly, setting her work aside.

Tsuguo, feeling her gaze fixed on him, swallowed nervously and asked, 'What year, month and day is it today?'

The cause of his nervousness was twofold.

The first was simple: *Will she think I'm strange for asking something like this?*

It was the kind of peculiar question you might hear from an amnesiac in a film or drama. If he asked it in a normal cafe, he would almost certainly be thought of as odd. That worried him. But then again, this was a cafe where one could travel to the past – surely it would be OK. That was the conclusion he had reached.

The second reason was different: *Dad isn't here . . . does that mean . . .?*

This was not so much worry as disappointment. The cafe was small, with three tables and a counter. From where he sat, he could see the entire room and at that moment, only he and Kazu were there.

It felt certain: *I won't be able to meet Dad.*

A complex blend of regret, sadness, and loneliness swirled within him. To Tsuguo's question, Kazu replied, 'It's the eighth of November 2018.'

For a moment, Tsuguo doubted his ears. Ryutaro had said he'd eaten a delicious carbonara when Tsuguo was in fourth grade. If that was true, Ryutaro would have visited this cafe in 2015 for the timeline to make sense.

'2018? Really?' Tsuguo was so shaken he almost rose from his seat.

'Yes. I'm certain,' Kazu replied, and resumed her work.

What . . .?

Tsuguo's mind was in turmoil. November 2018 was six months before Ryutaro's death. By then, carbonara no longer appeared on the dinner table as often as it had.

'Um.'

'Yes?'

'I – I visualized it. When you told me to picture my father coming to this cafe. Well, to be precise, I didn't actually know if he ever came here, but you told me to visualize it anyway, so I did. But . . . I seem to have come to a completely wrong day, and, um, so . . .'

Shaken, Tsuguo began to confuse the Kazu standing before him with the Kazu from the future who had made his coffee. Trying to explain everything at once, he only tied himself in knots.

Kazu, however, seemed to understand perfectly what the bewildered boy was saying.

'Then I believe you've come to the very time you pictured.'

'The time I pictured?'

'Yes.'

With that, she abruptly went back into the kitchen.

Taken aback by her sudden departure, Tsuguo sat in uneasy silence and let his eyes wander about the cafe. He was in a fluster – but not because of Kazu. He simply had no idea what to do.

What did I do wrong? She told me to imagine Dad being here, so that's what I pictured. But maybe I needed to imagine a specific time too? Oh . . . come to think of it, didn't she say something like, 'If the image of him never having come here is stronger, then even if he did, you'll return to a day when he wasn't in the cafe'? Maybe somewhere in my heart, I imagined he'd never been here . . . And if Father never came to the cafe, then whether it's 2018 or 2015 doesn't matter anyway . . .

He recalled Nagare's words: 'If there's even a chance to gain that kind of happiness, why not take it?'

No reason to regret trying. Even if I can't meet Dad, nothing about the future will change. Life will go on just as before. If I could meet him, I'd be happy – that's all. If Dad never came to this cafe – that's disappointing – but there's nothing I can do about it.

He took a deep breath and exhaled slowly, trying to steady himself. As calm returned, he noticed the pristine white cup before him.

Time to go.

He reached for the cup.

At that moment, a familiar voice came from the kitchen.

'Tsuguo?'

Turning around towards the kitchen, Tsuguo saw Ryutaro standing there.

The sudden sight of his father left him speechless, completely stunned, as Ryutaro walked towards him.

'What are you doing here, in a place like this?'

Over a shirt, sleeves rolled up, he wore a reddish-brown kitchen apron tied around his waist. Though surprised, his expression softened into a warm smile.

'What about you, Dad . . .?'

The words slipped out reflexively, but Tsuguo's mind hadn't yet caught up with the situation.

'I . . . well, the owner here was teaching me how to make a really good carbonara . . .' Ryutaro muttered awkwardly, scratching his head.

'But that was . . . years ago . . .'

'Years ago? Ah – yeah, the carbonara I made then was really good too, wasn't it? I remember you loving it. But the carbonara here? It's even better. It's insanely good. I thought I had to let you try it too, so I asked for the recipe, but just having the recipe wasn't enough to make it taste right. So the owner said, "I'll teach you," and . . .'

'Is that your son?' came Nagare's voice from behind Ryutaro.

'Ah, yes.'

Ryutaro turned to introduce Tsuguo to Nagare.

'This is my son, Tsuguo. He loves carbonara, don't you? Go on, say hello.'

'Er, yeah.'

At Ryutaro's prompting, Tsuguo almost stood up without thinking. But Nagare quickly raised a hand to stop him.

'Ah – stay seated!'

'Oh . . .'

Tsuguo immediately realized what Nagare meant. If he stood up, he would be forcibly pulled back into the future. He relaxed and sat back on the chair.

'But—'

'It's fine. Besides, your son's probably here for something important, isn't he? I'll keep an eye on the pasta I'm boiling, so go ahead.'

With that, Nagare vanished into the kitchen before Ryutaro could even reply. Kazu followed him.

Now only Tsuguo and Ryutaro remained in the cafe.

Tsuguo sat there, still shaken to be face to face with Ryutaro, who was supposed to have died four months earlier.

It really is Dad.

Tsuguo couldn't bring himself to look directly at his face. The man sitting before him wasn't the lifeless, waxen figure he'd seen in the coffin on the day of the funeral. This Ryutaro was just as he remembered – healthy and warm, with a smile on his face. Tsuguo fought desperately to hold back the tears threatening to spill.

'I'm surprised you knew about this place. Did I ever tell you about it?' Ryutaro said as he lowered himself into the seat opposite his son.

Tsuguo kept his head down, unable to lift his gaze.

'Hmm? What's the matter? Something bothering you?'

Ryutaro leaned in, peering at his son's downcast face with

concern. Normally, Tsuguo would speak up on his own, but today, he was uncharacteristically silent.

'Ah, no . . . it's nothing.'

'That so?'

'Yeah.'

'Wait a second. Don't tell me—'

'What?'

'You've got a girl you like, haven't you?'

'Huh?'

'So you've reached that age, eh? So, what's she like? Is she in your class?'

'No, it's not like that.'

'Come on, don't lie.'

'I told you. That's not it!'

'Then what is it? What's with that face?'

Ryutaro pursed his lips as if to say, *You usually tell me everything.* That familiar gesture, so ordinary in their past life together, stirred Tsuguo's emotions all the more.

I can't cry here.

Tsuguo bit down hard on his lip.

'Dad.'

'Hm?'

I can at least say what I promised myself I'd say if I ever got the chance to see him again.

Tsuguo touched his cup, checking its warmth.

A little lukewarm, but the alarm hadn't gone off yet.

He raised his head and began.

'Dad, there's something I need to tell you.'

'What is it? You're awfully serious . . .'

Ryutaro straightened up, confused by the rare earnestness in his son's voice and expression. Still, there was a hint of his usual easy-going air in his eyes, as though he half expected a surprise. To Tsuguo, this was a reunion after four long months, but to Ryutaro, it felt like they'd been together just that morning.

After Tsuguo spoke, he fell silent again, staring down at the table. Ryutaro, growing impatient, leaned in.

'What is it? This isn't like you. Is it that hard to say?' The silence continued. 'If not today, then—'

'I've met Mum,' Tsuguo said.

'What?' Ryutaro froze for several seconds. Then at last, he murmured, 'I see . . .'

Leaning back in his chair, he stared blankly at the ceiling. The easy-going father who had been joking about crushes just moments ago was gone. His eyes were clouded with shock and confusion.

Tsuguo's mother had fallen into postpartum depression shortly after giving birth. She had abandoned both father and son, vanishing from their lives. But Ryutaro had never blamed her.

Postpartum depression can happen to anyone. It wasn't her fault.

That's what he had always told himself.

He'd never spoken ill of her to Tsuguo, partly because he'd thought – hoped – that one day she might come back and ask to be part of her son's life.

But hearing from Tsuguo himself that he had met his mother without Ryutaro knowing was a far greater shock than he could have imagined. Had she come to him first, said she wanted to see her son, and let him bring the two of them together, he might have been ready for it. But to find out it had already happened . . .

A flicker of anger towards her rose in his chest. Yet more than that, he was anxious for his son's next words. Now he understood why Tsuguo had seemed so tense and distant.

If it's this hard for him to say, then . . . it must be what I think it is.

Ryutaro had no choice but to wait.

I don't want to hear it. But my son has found the courage to tell me something important. As his father, I can't turn away. If I'm not ready to listen, Tsuguo won't be able to speak either.

Quietly, so Tsuguo wouldn't notice, Ryutaro drew a deep breath and asked, 'And?'

'Er, yeah . . . Mum asked if I'd like to live with her.'

'I see.'

'She kept saying "I'm sorry, I'm so sorry."'

'You heard everything, then?'

'Yeah,' Tsuguo muttered, clenching his fists tight.

'Thank you . . . for never saying anything bad about Mum, even up till today.'

'Yeah.'

After that, silence fell between them. Tsuguo kept his head down, while Ryutaro stared at the ceiling fan turning slowly above them.

The sound of the alarm brought Tsuguo back to himself. He touched the cup with his hand.

Ah . . .

The coffee had cooled to the point that he could drink it in one gulp. Even so, he held back.

I still haven't said what's really important.

Meanwhile, Ryutaro, mistaking the alarm for the signal that the pasta was ready, said, 'Has it boiled?'

He stood up abruptly and turned his back on Tsuguo.

'Dad!'

Ryutaro froze mid-step, still facing away, when Tsuguo called out to him.

'Er . . . um . . .'

Tsuguo was supposed to live with his mother. But that decision had come after Ryutaro's funeral, when Tsuguo finally accepted her request. Until Ryutaro died, he had never even considered living with his mother.

'The truth is . . . I . . . I turned her down.'

'What?'

'I'm going to stay with you for ever, Dad . . .'

It was a lie. Strictly speaking, it wasn't – at least not back when Ryutaro was alive. But after seeing the look on Ryutaro's face when he had mentioned meeting his mother, Tsuguo could no longer tell him he planned to live with her. And Tsuguo felt that was for the best.

When Ryutaro heard Tsuguo's words, he clenched his eyes shut. Raising his face, he bit his lip hard.

His shoulders trembled.

'I see.'

At last, tears welled and spilled from Ryutaro's eyes.

'You're really that happy?' Hiding his face, Ryutaro wiped the tears from his cheeks. 'Damn it, Tsuguo . . .'

'Ah, um . . . it's about time . . .'

Nagare suddenly called out from the kitchen. Of course, it was directed at Tsuguo – it was time for him to finish the coffee. But Ryutaro mistook it as being meant for him and replied, 'Ah, I'm coming!' He started towards the kitchen, flustered.

'Dad!'

Tsuguo's voice stopped him.

'Hm?'

'I'm looking forward to your carbonara.'

'Leave it to me.'

'OK.'

Ryutaro spun around, but for some reason, he didn't head to the kitchen. Instead, he remained standing there. Tsuguo was puzzled why his father was lingering, but he needed to do what he had to do. He tipped the coffee back and drained it in one go.

At once, a wave of dizziness washed over him.

Ah . . . good. I made it in time.

He looked up. Ryutaro was still standing motionless.

'Dad?'

'Thank you, Tsuguo.'

Ryutaro murmured a little awkwardly, his back still turned.

'Yeah . . .'

The very next moment, Tsuguo's body dissolved into a thin veil of white, drawn upward toward the ceiling.

November 2019

'Move!'

When he came to his senses, Tsuguo found the woman in the white dress standing in front of him.

'Ah, I'm sorry!'

He stood hurriedly and gave up his seat to her.

'Dad?'

He glanced around the cafe, then called out to the kitchen.

There was no reply.

Was it just a dream?

The strange experience of meeting his late father made Tsuguo even doubt his own memory. Yet when he closed his eyes, he could still clearly recall Ryutaro's expression, his voice, and every word they had exchanged. Even if it had been a dream, it felt like a moment of happiness.

After a while, Kazu appeared from the kitchen, carrying a freshly brewed coffee for the woman in the white dress.

Tsuguo noticed that her hair, tied back, was longer than before. It had reached only her shoulders earlier, but now it flowed down her back.

Good. It wasn't a dream.

He reached for the coat draped over his chair.

CLANG-DONG

The entrance bell rang as Nagare returned, Miki in tow. Seeing Tsuguo's face, he asked, 'Did you meet him?'

'Yes.'

'I see. That's good.'

'Thank you very much.'

Nagare was clearly pleased that Tsuguo and Ryutaro had been reunited, though he seemed puzzled about why he couldn't remember Ryutaro visiting the cafe.

'But why don't I remember him coming in?'

'Ah, that's because . . .'

Tsuguo went on to explain that Ryutaro's visit had been last year, and after that, Nagare had taught him how to make carbonara.

'Ah! Ryutaro! Yes, yes! Now I remember – he did come in!'

Nagare nodded, satisfied that everything made sense now.

CLANG-DONG

As he had when he arrived, Tsuguo bowed politely to Nagare and Kazu before leaving the cafe.

That night

A message arrived on Kazu's phone. It was from Koku, letting her know he had arrived in France.

Attached was a photograph of Jumièges Abbey, known as the most awe-inspiring ruin in France. But unlike the work photos he usually sent – empty, silent landscapes – this one was a selfie with Koku himself in the frame.

He had always sent her selfies from wherever he travelled. This time, however, his message included a single line:

Someday, please marry me.

Koku.

Until now, Kazu had never replied to any of Koku's emails or messages. She had never felt the need to.

But on this day, for the first time, Kazu sent him a reply:

I'll think about it.

Kazu Tokita.

Their time, too, was moving forward moment by moment.

More than 2 million copies sold worldwide

Before the Coffee Gets Cold
Series

In a charming Tokyo cafe, customers are offered the unique experience of time-travel. But there are rules and the journey does not come without risks. Customers must return to the present before the coffee gets cold . . .

Translated from Japanese by Geoffrey Trousselot, Toshikazu Kawaguchi's heartwarming and wistful series tells the stories of people who must face up to their past in order to move on with their lives.

What would you do if you could travel back in time?